Lullabies for Satan

Ben Docherty

Lullabies for Satan

Vanguard Press

VANGUARD PAPERBACK

A CIP catalogue record for this title is
available from the British Library.

ISBN 978 1 80016 953 1

Vanguard Press is an imprint of
Pegasus Elliot Mackenzie Publishers Ltd.
www.pegasuspublishers.com

First Published in 2024

Vanguard Press
Sheraton House Castle Park
Cambridge England

Printed & Bound in Great Britain

To Mum,
who would not have approved of the language or contents of this book.

Zenash — for support and editing.
Dom — he spotted a mistake and was very happy about it.

1

The devil has trouble sleeping. He never understood why, and over the last millennia or so it had started to affect his work. This was a problem as his job was fairly important, even though he had several generals who had several sergeants who had thousands of minions; his day-to-day was packed full of paperwork, admin, and meetings regarding the ever-changing policies of heaven and hell and the general business of caretaking human souls.

Perhaps what annoyed him most was his co-worker, God, and his insatiable propensity for sleeping like a baby. God could often be found napping, and often on the job, which was why bad things were constantly happening to good God-fearing people of the world. Every now and then he takes a lethal dose (or at least it would be lethal for mortals), of morphine and he can't be reached for days or even weeks, meanwhile natural disasters savage the world beneath.

God had held his position as creator — in reality he was the son of the creator, but his ego wouldn't let him acknowledge that — for a long while. He took over from his father roughly two millennia ago and immediately screwed the pooch by unleashing his son on the world tens of thousands of years before they were ready for such a thing. That's where nepotism gets you in the realm of the divine. Meanwhile, the devil toiled away and kept his head down and worked harder than anyone else in the many echelons of hell and was rightly put in charge of caring for the evil of the, then brand new, species of humans. And for the last two million years or so, he hasn't slept.

Paramount to this affliction was the popular belief among the living that he was an evil being and is often labelled as the antichrist. It perplexed him (or rather, pissed him off) that he was constantly being mistaken for the devil depicted in many religious texts, which represent the abstract concept of evil, wrongdoing and temptation. When, in reality, he was just a being with a job to do. As if he even had time to visit earth and tempt good willing humans off the path of righteousness never mind the compulsion to do so.

At a seminar held in heaven, the devil finally decided to speak to the man who seemed like he had it all figured out, God.

"God, hey how's it going?" he tentatively opened.

"Hey man, how's things at the bottom of existence?" God casually replied, sipping a Mai tai.

"Yeah, it's, uh, it's busy you know."

"Oh man, tell me about it," God assented with a vigorous nod of his head.

"You've been busy too?"

"No man, we got fuck all going on. People these days man, they're all fucking sinners, that's why I figure you must busy cause I sure as shit ain't," God said.

"Right, right, yeah," the devil replied suppressing the impulse to scorn.

"This one guy man, we had our eye on him for a while, real peaceful dude you know, like, at one with nature and shit. Anyway, he was meditating in the forest next to a lake somewhere outside Tibet, just, like, waiting to die you know, and we're all ready to welcome him to eternal paradise and shit, and then out of nowhere, this stunning babe, like a college chic or something, walks by, strips butt-naked and goes for a swim. Now the Tibetan dude is trying real hard not to pay attention to her, but you know, they're in a forest what the fuck else is going on, so he looks up and she starts enticing him into the fucking lake man!" God starts laughing so much he has to pause and put his drink down. He continues now talking with both hands waving enthusiastically, "So he starts walking towards the lake, stripping down, he's got an erection for the first time in years, you know the guy's like eighty, and he drops dead of a heart attack before he even gets his toe in."

"And that's all it takes, no heaven?"

"Impure thoughts man, coveting, desire, impulses beyond their fucking control and they end up with you. It's bullshit if you ask me, but hey, more work for you less for me right?" God jokingly punches the devil on the shoulder at this taunt. The devil, rubbing his shoulder, says,

"How do you sleep at night?" Attempting to put it out there as a jest but God sees through it and looks at him thoughtfully.

"Shit, man, you having problems at home?"

"Well, you know…"

"Fuck, you can tell me man."

"I haven't slept well in a while I guess, or at all really," the devil mutters this last part, staring at the ground.

"Shit, no wonder, it's so fucking warm down there I was damn near sweating my balls clean off last time. You should get some fucking air-conditioning or some shit down there. I mean for fuck's sake man *humans* have it, and they're fucking mortal, you're the fucking devil man!"

"Yeah, I think it might be more than that, I'm used to the heat by now."

"Well shit man, sounds like you got some real problems, maybe you should try praying, huh?" God punches the devil's shoulder again at this taunt. "Oh shit there's Loki, I fucking love that guy he's always tripping, hey see you later man, and for Christ's sake take it easy, huh?" And with that God left the devil standing at the buffet table, alone, no further along in seeking a solution and more pissed off than when he started. He stared after God, letting his hatred grow as he remembers the fact that God has never apologised for the humans releasing a book that praises God and talks shit about him for thousands of pages. *Fucking humans*, he thought to himself as Loki and God ran off to another room, to ingest the latest psychedelics Loki had retrieved from the far reaches of the universe.

2

Peter was a musician. Not a successful one, but how many actually are? Peter reconciled this with the knowledge that he was incredibly talented and the belief that he was unlucky. He was old enough now to realise that, while luck played a part, his own bad decisions and lack of motivation also played a major role in his current situation.

Sat at his Petite Grand piano, Peter wiped some dust off the top, noticing the many rings left by coffee mugs, and considered his current situation. It wasn't all bad, he may be divorced but it was better than being married. He stayed in a meagre studio flat, but it wasn't on the bottom floor. He wasn't successful, but he had work. On balance, Peter would consider himself, content.

The cat jumped on the end of the piano, crashing a few keys. The outburst brought Peter back to the present. His current commission came from his cousin, who worked at an ad agency in London and occasionally threw Peter some lower importance work out of pity. It wasn't the most inspiring of projects, but it paid the bills. Usually, Peter quite enjoyed the tedium of these tasks, and the comfort of low expectation, but today, something was off. Something in the back of his head told him he was never going to finish this project, that there wasn't any point.

Then the phone rang. Peter knew it was Karen, he knew by the way phone rang, it was uncomfortable and aggressive. Karen didn't have his mobile number, so Peter often thought of ripping the phone out the wall and throwing it away, but it was the only way his parents could contact him. Begrudgingly, Peter left the piano and answered the phone.

"Yes, hello?"

"Peter, it's Karen."

"Yeah, I figured, what's up?"

"Can you send the money early this month?"

"What? No, I don't have it." The cat was staring at him from the couch, with its head cocked to the side, the way a dog does when its curious. Peter frowned at the cat and tried to shoo it away.

"C'mon Peter don't be a dick about this."

"How the fuck am I being dick, we have an arrangement in place. I haven't missed a payment in years, and I made up for that."

"Look, I didn't call you for an argument."

"The fuck you didn't. I don't have time for this."

"Oh really, you got a big project on the go?" The sarcasm vibrated through the phone line and rattled Peter's jaw.

"Fuck you very much, Karen." Peter slammed the phone down. The cat, unmoved, was still staring at him. It wasn't even his, had no collar, just turned up every now and again and Peter fed it. He didn't bother to name it, if anyone ever asked, he just referred to it as 'the cat'.

"Thank fuck we didn't have kids," Peter thought aloud to the empty room. He often consoled himself with this thought after dealing with Karen, aside from any child support issues, the idea of raising a child that was half *hers* made his blood boil.

Sitting back down at the piano, Peter closed his eyes and took a deep breath in, and out. He opened his eyes and tried to lift his arm to turn the music sheet. Confusion spread across his rough, unshaved face as his body went numb and he slumped to the floor, the keys of the piano giving a quick tune as it hopped up and down from the impact. Peter lay motionless on the floor as the cat came over and began nudging him, looking for some food.

3

Balthazar awoke with a start. Satan was calling him again. The ringing in his head wasn't loud but the sound was violent, and the fire burned bright behind his eyes letting him know the urgency of the call. This had been happening more and more often recently and at increasingly odd times of the night. Satan had been having trouble sleeping and as much as Balthazar felt bad for the guy, as well as how much he liked and respected the boss, it had started to piss him off. Just because he couldn't get some shut eye didn't mean he had the right to interrupt everyone else at any fucking time of his choosing.

Balthazar sat up in his bed, sighed heavily and looked around his room. The rock walls were jagged and unwelcoming, the sulphur burned bright blue, filling his nostrils with an unholy stench. It was modestly sized at best, enough space for himself and the occasional… guest. He loved the place. It was his and his alone. No one could interfere with his space, his home, he could recognise it blindfolded, one touch of any rock or stone in the room and he knew he was back where he belonged.

There was only one thing that could penetrate this fortress — that fucking alarm. And it was ringing now. There were downsides to being the devil's right-hand man. Time to go to work.

Heather was on reception again today. Balthazar hadn't decided if he liked her not, she was new and she was human, two of the most suspicious things you can be in the spiritual realm, especially here down below.

"Good morning Heather. You're looking fine today. Well, as fine as one could look when you're just bone and muscle covered in skin." Balthazar was joking with Heather, but he did genuinely consider humans to be ugly.

"Charming as always Balthazar."

"The big man called me. I assume he's in?"

"Indeed."

"Can you let him know I'm here?"

"He is leader of the Underworld; I think he already knows."

"Well then what the fuck is the point in you. Just… just fucking ring him, I'm in absolutely no mood for your shit today!" Heather stared down Balthazar, maintaining eye contact and scowling at him as she buzzed the intercom.

"Sir, Balthazar is here." Satan crackled inaudibly over the intercom. "He said to go right ahead."

"I don't know how the fuck you managed to convince him that this cut-rate human technology was a better system than the one we already had."

"You're keeping him waiting," Heather said snidely.

"Fuck you Heather." Balthazar walked away from Heather's desk. He had just now decided, he didn't like her, he *really* didn't like her. Not one single human would have the balls to speak to him like that if they didn't have the protection of the big man. Fucking bitch.

Balthazar walked into Satan's office, knocking as he did so.

"Hello? Sir?" He continued into the office to find Satan frantically pacing around and throwing pieces of paper on the floor as he did so.

"Sir? What's going on?"

"I've got it. I've fucking got it Zar, I swear to you this is the answer." Only the big man could call him 'Zar', an underling tried it once and promptly found himself tied to a cliff face, strung up by his scrotum.

"What are you talking about sir?" Satan was still rushing around the room, making Balthazar uneasy; he had seen him only occasionally flustered, but never in a manic state such as this.

"I just need one, but I can't fucking find any!" Satan screamed, as he tossed the remaining papers in his hands into the air.

"OK, sir, breath, relax. Take a seat and tell me what's happening." Satan did as Balthazar suggested, looking at him for the first time since he came into the office. Once he had calmed himself, he sat down at his throne. 'Throne' was its official name, but it was a simple chair, perhaps slightly larger than those afforded to others but hardly worthy of such a grandiose title. Apparently, the previous boss had a massive throne, lavishly decorated with skulls and fire and live snakes — all rumour of course — but this boss was far more professional and modest, and he didn't want to come across as too superior to those that worked for him.

The devil steadied himself, looked at Balthazar in the eye and began to explain.

"Music." He let the word hang in the air between them as if it explained everything by itself.

"Yes sir, what about it?"

"It's the key, they use it up there." They often referred to the realm of the living as 'up there' despite the fact it was not geographically located anywhere with respect to the realm of the dead and was instead on another astral plane.

"There's something about certain types of music or specific tunes or notes or whatever, they trigger something in the brain chemistry, and they help you sleep. I think this is it, I think this is what I need. I just can't find a bloody musician anywhere in our files."

"Sir, I'm not sure I follow, we don't have brain waves, at least not in the way that humans..."

"Yes, I know that!" Satan snapped. "But I'm at my wits' end. This must be it. This has to be how it works." Satan stared down Balthazar. Balthazar knew that he wasn't trying to convince him, he was trying to convince himself. So, Balthazar decided to indulge, at least for now.

"OK then. So, we need a musician. There's obviously plenty down here but if you want them to work for you then we need to actually own their soul."

"I know that, I've been looking, but I can't find anyone that has any notoriety. I thought musicians sold their souls to us all the time for fame and fortune? What the hell happened?"

"Well, I believe standards have dropped nowadays. Plus, with the advent of the internet and social media, there's no longer any need to sell your soul to us. Just put whatever shite you want on the web and wait for stardom, however fleeting it may be."

"Fuck me. Then what about the older ones?"

"As I'm sure you know sir, any souls we have that have been here for any more than a year will have withered away too much to be of any use to us. We need a fresh one." Satan sat back in his throne and sighed. "However, we don't need notoriety, nor fame. We just need talent, the two don't often go hand in hand." Satan leaned forward buoyed by Balthazar's words.

"Interesting, go on."

"Well, there are plenty of so-called failed musicians out there that haven't had any commercial success but had the potential to do so. If, and I mean *if*, we can find one of them, fresh, whose soul we own, then they might be able to do the trick."

"You think we'll have someone like that? It seems strange that someone who sold their soul to us wouldn't have achieved what they were looking for."

"You forget sir, since the invention of marriage, spouses own each other's souls. At least for the duration of the marriage. And divorce does not nullify any arrangement that a spouse has made with us for their partner's soul."

"So, what are you saying."

"I'm saying, all we need is a scornful ex. That shouldn't be too hard to find."

4

Peter was sat in the booth of a café, mindlessly stirring his tea. He was mesmerised by the motion, the swirling, rhythmic waves created by the sweeping movement of his spoon. It was so perfectly circular, no breaks in the liquid no ebb and flow or change of pace, just a very satisfying whirl of energy, seemingly effortless as the spoon made no sound and faced no friction.

A figure appeared and sat opposite Peter in the booth.

"Hello, Peter." Peter looked up from his tea and took in the strange apparition that sat across him. He was tall, striking, and broad shouldered with a rough, jagged face like an old, stereotyped fisherman.

"Hi." Peter offered a meek response with more than a little confusion in his voice.

"Where do you think you are right now Peter?" the figure asked.

"I… uh…" Taken aback, Peter looked around him for the first time. The café was quiet, with very few patrons and little life to the place. Everyone was moving slowly and barely interacting. There was nothing in the air, no smells, no atmosphere, and Peter realised for the first time that he had no idea where he was or how he got here. “I… I don’t know.”

“Understandable. Allow me to explain—” the figure started but Peter interrupted.

“Wait, how do you know my name? Who are you?” Peter continued to look around him for some clue of what was going on.

“Well, if you’ll give me a fucking second, I’ll explain all that. I get you’re a little confused, but I don’t appreciate the attitude. Any more of that and I’ll put you straight back.”

“Back where? What—” Peter stammered into further questions, but he was silenced by the figure who simply raised his hand. Transfixed by the large, commanding hand of the figure, Peter noticed out the corner of his eye that what little movement there had been in the café had ceased altogether, as if the figure had stopped time simply with his annoyance.

“Peter… you’re dead. You’ve been dead for a few months now. You’re currently in hell. In hell your consciousness is stored in a sort of ‘pool’ where you slowly wither away in pain and misery until there’s nothing left. I’ve taken you out of that pool and allowed your consciousness to take a human form. You may now react to that information and I will try to answer any questions you may have.”

Peter sat dumbfounded, attempting to process all that this stranger had just told him. Part of him knew it was true, that he was dead, his last memory was of feeling unwell in his living room, like he was about to faint. The café had sprung back to life, without Peter noticing, as his brain began to pick holes in the stranger's story, as if his own conscious activity were driving the life around him.

Peter began to quiz the stranger, "But you're saying that—"

"My name is Balthazar," Balthazar was quick to interrupt.

"Right, Balthazar, sure, whatever, you're saying that in this 'hell pool' I'm conscious, but my last memory is of me alive in my living room?"

"Sure, for the sake of your sanity, I've wiped any memory of hell from your consciousness."

"Um… OK." Peter sat back and thought once again. He ran his hand through his hair, feeling the sensation of the hair flowing between his fingers. His hand drifted in front of his face and Peter instinctively inspected it, turning it over and examining both sides carefully. It was then that the tea sitting in front of him came into focus. Peter picked up the mug and swirled the tea around, staring into it as if maybe there were answers somewhere to be found in the murky brown liquid.

Peter looked up at Balthazar and motioned to the tea, "Is this even real?"

Balthazar shrugged. "Have you tried it?" Peter looked down at the tea and raised his eyebrows in curiosity. First, he gave the mug a quick sniff, then took a sip. It tasted, undoubtedly, like tea. Peter's curiosity quickly turned to confusion and he threw his hands up in exacerbation.

“OK, so how the fuck does that work?”

Balthazar perked up at his question and shot Peter a finger to give him props. “Now that, is a mighty fine question. I think we’re getting somewhere.”

5

The devil awoke with the sensation of falling. His cold, fiery heart was bursting out his chest and he was almost panting. Gripping the sides of his bed he looked around his chamber to confirm that he was still in hell. There was a brief moment of relief as he recognised the bare, rock walls and minimalist design of blue fire and brimstone, but it was quickly replaced by yet another panic as he realised that in order to wake up you have to fall asleep! Checking his Universal Realm Watch he began to get excited that perhaps he had a full sleep, but alas, only five human minutes had passed since he had drifted off and his rude awakening had occurred far too soon.

Balthazar was currently working on the musician's soul and had said that he may be ready before the working day began, but these things can take time and they had never retrieved one that had spent so much time in hell already. The devil began to pace as doubt creeped into his mind like darkness creeps onto the earth at sunset. This human has no reason to trust them and even if he does, with no incentive, why in hell would he help them. They couldn't threaten him with anything that they weren't going to do to him anyway, unless they lied, but with no possible follow through that was far too risky. The simple truth was that they had nothing to offer, they couldn't send him back to earth and they couldn't ascend him to heaven either. This was tricky at the best of times but with God firmly putting the wall up to even the best of humanity, it was damn impossible.

A flash of inspiration told The devil he should speak to Heather. First off, she had the file on the human, and it would be wise to learn more about him before any meeting. Secondly, Heather was the most recent soul they had brought to their dimensional plane, so perhaps he could learn more about what the Human was going through. Information is a weapon.

6

Heather was sitting at her desk (which was too small to be comfortable, one of the many micro-aggressions designed to piss her off) with her head in her hands, looking outwards at the fiery pits. It was almost homely, with a certain cosy aesthetic that would be comforting if it wasn't for the atmosphere. It had a foreboding, eerie sense of dread that just hung in the air, you couldn't see it or necessarily feel it, but it was undoubtedly there, reminding everyone present that this is not a place meant for the humankind, or any kind that normally calls earth home. In her past life, Heather had been a vet, a love of animals from a young age had managed to persist through the nihilistic teenage years and extended all the way to adulthood where it led her to veterinary school. Now she was here, her role as a secretary was all part of the punishment. As a working professional she hated the stereotype of the woman assistant, it was a fine job to do but it was the assumption that bothered her. No one who ever came across her desk here questioned her position for a moment.

During her quiet musing, Heather received a distressful call from the boss. The call system they had in place meant that when she was buzzed, the buzz reflected the nature of the call. Ordinarily, the buzz was chilled and easy, almost morose, but lately they had become more… frantic. Heather entered the office to see the boss sat at the front of his desk, stroking his goatee and gently tapping his goat leg. She knew this was not his real form and simply the one that her conscious had come up with, as Balthazar had first explained, but it was still comical to see this caricature as the leader of the underworld.

"Can I help you sir?" Heather began, she normally waited for him to speak first, but he had been silent for a long time since she had entered.

"What can you tell me about this person, this musician. You have his file, right?" He didn't look at her as he spoke, didn't even lift his head. Heather understood this was just the mood he was in, but it was another one of the million things that added to her pain.

"No sir, I must have left it by the pool while I was drinking cocktails." The boss chuckled and finally looked up.

"Nice one, OK give it to me." He held out his hand and Heather handed over the file. She hated playing the role of the sarcastic, sassy black woman. The alternative was to go back to the pit. At first, she had no memory of it, but once she started to disobey and speak up for herself, Balthazar had slowly replanted the memories, not enough for her to lose her sanity but just enough to keep her in check. So, she played the part. The boss thumbed through the papers that Heather had given him.

"So, his ex hates him, that's not exactly unique." He muses as he draws a scaley finger down the paper.

"No, but in this case, she never liked him. At the time they met he was trending upwards and was on his way to some success. She wanted to get out from under her parents but didn't want to work for it, so she saw him as a ticket," Heather explained, she always had a knack for remembering information. It came in handy when studying for exams, now it was being used to help torture people. "Once it became apparent that he wasn't going anywhere she sold his soul, left him and still continued to take his money."

"Child support?"

"No, they had no children."

"Impotent?"

"No, she asked him to get a vasectomy and he did."

"Interesting… interesting…" the boss trailed off, he began looking *through* the paper rather than at it and you could see the cogs of his twisted mind doing overtime.

"So… what's it like?" At this he looked up, directly at Heather, as he set the file down on his desk.

"What's what like?" Heather was bemused, not only because she didn't know what he was referring to but also because she never gets asked personal questions of any nature.

"Coming back. From the…" the boss trailed off again, this time from discomfort, not distraction. Heather finished for him,

"From the pit of unending despair?"

"That's not its name, and it's not unending, it does end."

"It's… strange. It feels wrong, like you shouldn't be here, like you don't belong. But at the same time, you don't know where you do belong. So, there's just this cycle of not wanting to be anywhere, a constant sense of dread and longing to stop existing altogether."

"Interesting." Heather could see from his expression that he was trying to figure out how to use this information, rather than giving a single fuck that this is how Heather feels every day. She found herself disappointed in her disappointment, this was the literal fucking devil and yet some small part of her still believed that he gave a damn. Suppose he has his own problems, can't be easy being an insomniac when you're responsible for the entire Underworld.

The boss snapped out of his thinking and gave a heavy sigh. "That'll be all Heather."

Heather left and returned to her desk. Knowing he would never say thank you, knowing she would never be respected or cared for, knowing that this existence was all there was and all there will ever be, the only sense of solace she had was in realising that how she is treated here isn't too dissimilar to the land of the living.

7

Balthazar and Peter had been talking for some time now. Progress was slow as Peter struggled to come to terms with his new reality. Despite Balthazar's best efforts, Peter had only just got to grips with the existence of hell and the pool of souls from which he had recently been liberated. Peter now turned his attention to Balthazar himself.

"So, you're a demon?"

"Correct," Balthazar replied with an air of accomplishment and a grin of superiority.

"I guess I never thought demons took… human form." Peter gestured broadly at Balthazar's appearance.

"Ah, well we don't, I'm appearing to you in a way that you feel is palatable. I have no idea how I currently look to you. The truth is your mortal brain couldn't comprehend my true form."

"I'm confused again."

"Of course you are, look, if I walk in here looking like an actual fucking demon then your synapses will cease to synapse, or whatever the fuck they normally do. So, we have a sort of filter."

"Like Instagram or something."

"Don't fucking start with that shit. I am an ageless mystical entity not some gimmicky fucking nonsense that lets teenagers look like fairies or some shit. As far as you're concerned, I'm a fucking god. So that's the last time you compare any part of me to a fucking tool." Peter was taken aback by Balthazar's genuine fury. Up until now he had an air of indifference, a laid-back 'I don't give a fuck' attitude that Peter had become comfortable with. This was a stark reminder not to mess around.

"OK, understood, won't happen again." Peter began damage control. "Back to it though, how can you not know what you look like to me?"

"Like I said, I'm appearing in a way that you, as in you personally, find palatable. If I were to guess I'd say that I'm a man, seeing as you're generally uncomfortable around all women. I'd also guess that I'm white seeing as you're a white man from a certain generation in the western world—"

"Hey, I'm not—"

"Never said you were, interesting that you immediately got defensive though. It's a given I'm speaking English. I'd also say that I'm taller and more attractive than you seeing as you're more comfortable being the beta in all of your relationships." Balthazar let his analysis hang in the air as Peter became demoralised at how quickly, accurately, and most importantly, *succinctly* Balthazar had broken him down. "How'd I do?"

"No comment," Peter said after a few seconds of considering how to respond.

"Ha, 'no comment' is one hell of a comment, just for the record."

Peter rolled his eyes and once again looked around the café. He knew by now it wasn't real, but not on every level. The details were remarkable, the wallpaper was peeling from the edges, there were coffee stains on some of the tables and the colour on the countertops showed signs of decay. The whole place was run-down, and Peter considered if this mirrored what he had already lost in the 'pool'.

Peter turned back to Balthazar, who had begun picking at his nails — which he apparently didn't even know he had. His air of indifference had returned, but Peter could see his impatience growing. This had bothered him at first but now he didn't care. What exactly did he owe this being, this apparition? Perhaps he wasn't in hell at all, maybe this whole thing was a coma dream, and he was currently lying in a hospital bed with wires coming out of him. Peter tried to concentrate to see if he could hear the beeps of the machines or the distinctive smell of a hospital ward, but his senses were dead here. Perhaps he wasn't in a hospital ward but rather a psychiatric ward, maybe he had been his whole life, simply imagining his entire existence, and now this was all happening because they had changed his medication or something. It was all more probable than what he was being told by this unholy figure. The thoughts all swirled in his head like the tea in his cup when he stirred the spoon. Eventually Peter figured that whatever was going on, there was nothing he could do about it now, so he may as well learn some more about his current situation, even if it was just fever dream.

"You said I had been in that pool thing for a few months, withering away. What does that mean exactly? What have I already lost?" Balthazar focused in again and leaned forward on the table, clearly energised by this line of questioning.

"Great question Peter, well I'm sorry to be the one to tell you this but… you have no penis." Peter jumped up with wide-eyed horror and instinctively grabbed his crotch. Realising his penis was perfectly intact he sighed heavily and sat back down as Balthazar began laughing uncontrollably.

"Yes, very funny," Peter said dryly.

"You're all the fucking same, honestly, like that's the worst thing you could possibly think of isn't it? The truth is that you've lost some core memories, the very fabric of what makes you uniquely you. What makes up the very essence of your soul has been slowly dissolving. *That's* what you've lost. Albeit not that not much given you're relatively new here. Are you telling me you wouldn't trade a penis to have that back? It's not even your real penis, that's not your real body, and even if it was what the fuck are going to do with it down here? Dig a hole in the mud and fuck the ground?"

"Point taken." Peter considered what he had just been told, he had lost a small part of his soul, yet he didn't feel any different. Maybe he hadn't lost enough to feel a difference yet. Maybe he never had much of a soul to begin with. It was then that Peter had a stroke of inspiration, a moment of clarity, he looked up and straight at Balthazar.

"Wait a minute, why the fuck am I here anywhere?" asked Peter. Balthazar considered this heavily, inhaling deeply through his nose, gently rubbing his hands as his eyes wandered around.

"Yeah, I guess you're probably ready for this. I'm just going to come right out and say it, because honestly, it doesn't even make sense to me: the devil wants you to write him some music to help him sleep." Peter examined Balthazar's face for any sign of a wind-up, given his earlier prank Peter had learned to stop taking him at face value. However, he could see no crease in the face or glint in the eye of the figure opposite him.

"The devil? *The* devil? Wants lullabies?"

"The devil, Satan, Beelzebub, Prince of Darkness, whatever you want to call him, that's who he is. And yes, he's recently decided that music is the key to his insomnia."

"You guys can get insomnia? I didn't even realise you slept."

"He's just another being, doing a job. We all need some rest, even the ruler of the Underworld." Peter sat back and thought about the proposition, he felt somewhat empowered by the fact that he was needed for something, that he had a purpose now.

"So, what's in it for me?"

"Absolutely nothing, either you do it and then you go back in the pool, or you don't do it and you go back in the pool. You're going back either way, I'm giving you the chance to delay it slightly and exist, in a full form, for a while longer." This was not what Peter had wanted, or expected to hear. He refused to accept that his fate was inevitable, most rational people would. However, going back to the pool now was hardly an option, perhaps he could negotiate something later, after he had managed to gain some sway or leverage.

"All right then. I guess I could give it a go." Peter did not truly appreciate the absurdity of it all at this point in time, but he soon would. He had not thought about how he would go about this or how it could possibly work, all he cared about right now was getting the fuck out of this café. "So how do we get out of here?"

"That's simple, Peter," Balthazar leaned forward and held out his hands, "take my hands, and if you really believe, in your heart of hearts, then we can escape this place."

"For real?" Peter asked surprised.

"No, you fucking idiot." Balthazar took his hands away and sat upright. "We just walk out the fucking front door."

8

Tantalus liked to think of himself as a merry little trickster, a cheeky wee menace whispering sweet nothings into humans' ears, gently persuading them, guiding them towards what they have always believed but couldn't bring themselves to admit. None of this was true however, the truth was that Tantalus was just a cunt.

For millennia he has been in charge of sales, or rather, procurement. This requires a special listening device — known simply as the 'Receiver' — that allows him to hear whenever a human is considering selling their soul. Tantalus was happy enough with this gig to begin with. There were enough humans around the earth that kept him busy, and he revelled in seeing them come so close to rock bottom, so far into the darkness that they contemplated selling off their very essence just for a chance at a better life. It was laughable to Tantalus that these inferior beings thought so much of themselves and of their pitiful lives.

This contented Tantalus for a while, but he grew tired, restless, he needed more. As the humans advanced, they began seeking other outlets for their dire circumstances.

From life coaches and self-help books to tarot readers and astrology, the entire race was turning away from ethereal help.

Tantalus decided to take matters into his own idle hands. He discovered a way to reconfigure the 'Receiver.' Obviously, he still refers to it by this name, but unbeknownst to anyone, it could now transmit. So began Tantalus' reign as an angel of temptation. The little voice of self-doubt in your head, the devil on your shoulder telling you that it will *not* all be OK. Tantalus managed to stray many a soul from a straight path and the files began to stack. He was in the business of taking souls, and once again, business was booming.

The real kicker came a few centuries later, with the humans' creation of marriage. The fact that a human being can own another's soul opened up so many opportunities that Tantalus could barely contain himself. You see, convincing someone that they are worthless was surprisingly easy, the human race was notoriously weak after all, but convincing them to give up on someone else, someone they supposedly loved and cared for, that was the real challenge, and Tantalus accepted it with glee. Nothing made him happier than driving the proverbial wedge between a married couple, turning them against each other, slowly, subtly, with the precision of a surgeon until the moment came to strike. It wasn't always obvious which partner to push over the edge, on which side of the coin to focus his last bit of energy and give the final whisper, the final nudge, towards damnation. In some cases, though, it was clear as day. Like Peter and Karen, Tantalus had never had an easier call to make than with Peter and Karen.

9

Karen met Peter when they were both seventeen, he played keyboard in a band that her friend from high school had taken her to see. They both went backstage afterwards, 'backstage' being a rather grandiose term for the tiny, run-down green room with the cold air and the warm beer. They began talking and Peter did what young men do; talked about himself. He was waxing lyrical about his big plans, riding the band to a label before going solo and being the biggest pianist since… someone, Karen couldn't remember the name, and at the time, couldn't name a single pianist. Karen didn't particularly like Peter, but she liked his ambition.

They were married by twenty-four, Peter had proposed but only because Karen had threatened to leave if he didn't. By then, the band still hadn't kicked on like Peter had thought it would, and the timing wasn't good for him. On the other hand, he wasn't sure he could find another girlfriend on his personality alone, so he took the plunge. His original idea had been to wait until he had a little notoriety and then he would have his pick of the 'chicks' — as he liked to say back then. It wasn't his purest idea, but he was young and selfish that way. Now he had a dependant, someone to look after, and that meant finding some real work.

It was only two years later that Peter realised he and Karen didn't stand a chance. Of course, Karen had known for a lot longer, that spark they had that first night was gone, Peter's ambition had disappeared and was replaced by an unmistakable aura of contentment. That simply wouldn't do.

Karen couldn't say for sure when the voice in her head had first started to cast doubt on their relationship. Perhaps it had always been there, from the very first day, or at least since their wedding day. Initially she had been able to drown it out, and keep some semblance of faith, but as time wore on it became harder to ignore. It started to make more and more sense until it was all she could hear, all she could think — it was inevitable.

Karen had tried to remember the good times, but frankly there weren't many. What little she could remember were far outweighed by the bad. The shame she felt asking her parents for help when they moved into their first flat; the disappointment that they couldn't afford the first-hand car; the daily reminders of his inadequacy whenever she opened the fridge or the cupboard to find the off-brand, insert-shop-name-here own line of biscuits and bread and cereal. The whole idea was to marry *up*, social mobility and all that, but even her parents could afford fucking Kellogg's.

Karen had known for a long time that she was leaving Peter, long before he knew it. But it wasn't before she met Tantalus that she realised she had the option of fucking him over before she left. He had appeared in her room one day while Peter was out on a gig — she had stopped going to his gigs after they got married — despite not being aware of any other world never mind otherworldly beings, she was not afraid of the figure. He felt familiar, like she knew him. Earlier that night, after Peter had stormed out during a beratement from Karen, she had cursed the sky and wished to God Peter could spend eternity in hell. But God didn't answer the call, Tantalus did.

He didn't beat around the bush either, explaining within seconds that Karen had the power to sell his soul in return for a better life for herself.

"Seems a bit mad. Is that really the rule?" she asked.

"Indeed. Seems mental to me as well but I don't make the rules. I simply come to those who ask the question, and I tell them the answer," Tantalus explained, lying through his teeth.

"So, what kind of life could I get?" Karen asked, sitting up in bed, overjoyed that this opportunity had presented itself. It was unbelievable that marrying Peter had finally worked out how she had wanted. She had planned for success *through* him, but now she could get it *using* him. A grin spread across Tantalus' face, however, not one that Karen could perceive. It was demented, cruel, perverse.

"Whatever kind you want." Karen slowly sat back as her eyes darted back and forth trying to keep up with her own thoughts rattling around her twisted brain. The choices were endless, literally endless. Tantalus waited patiently, he had been working her for only a couple of years (ordinarily, it would take much longer), so he was more than content to wait a few more minutes for her imagination to take hold. The best part for Tantalus, which he neglected to inform Karen, was that she wouldn't remember any of this, and of course, Peter wouldn't know a thing about it. Tantalus would remember though; he remembered them all.

10

Peter settled into his new abode. Balthazar had dropped him off, and on his way out told him to get some rest before they got to work. Peter hadn't realised he needed rest in this world, but as Balthazar had said in the café, we all need rest.

Peter looked around his surroundings, it was exactly what he thought a 'room' in hell might look like; rocky interior, dull-red colours and a perceptible sense of foreboding. He wondered if this is actually what the place looked like or if it had some sort of filter, like with Balthazar. He had not thought to ask Balthazar before he had left. Peter's eyes scanned across the room till he saw it.

How could he have missed it? How did he not notice it as soon as he entered the room? Had it just appeared now? Peter physically shook his head to shake out the questions as he walked towards the Baby Grand piano in the corner of the room. He inspected it like he was in a car showroom, walking around it in a slow circle, taking in the shape, size, and colours. The shine was incredible; not at all like the dull, worn-down, scratched instrument that probably still sat back in the real world beside his decaying corpse. Unless of course the neighbours had reported the smell by now. *Bad idea*, Peter thought to himself, best not to think about that.

Running his finger across the fallboard, Peter felt a sense of excitement that was wholly unfamiliar to him. It had been years since he had felt this way while looking at a piano. He lifted the fallboard and inhaled deeply, smelling the keys. The white ivory shone, and the black keys rose sharply above them, begging to be played. *I should rest*, Peter thought. Balthazar had told him to, and he gave orders not suggestions. The temptation was too great however and Peter gingerly sat down on the stool, gently pressing the furthest left key. Hearing that high-pitched ding reverberate around the rocky room sent a small shiver down his spine.

Peter was transported to the heady days of his teens, the days when he would play for hours on end, when he would put The Doors on his record player and play along with Ray Manzarek using only his ear to get the melody. He was good, he'd long since forgotten that but today he was reminded. He was good at this. Peter played for a while, like he hadn't played for years, or possibly ever. Then it hit him. He wasn't here to play *Light my Fire*, he was here to write a lullaby for the devil. The fucking *devil*. It was absolutely ludicrous, only a madman could even dream of such a thing and yet here he was, living it. Well, not exactly *living* it.

Was this even possible? Peter wasn't sure he could write a lullaby for a normal being. He'd read about it. How there's something in the melody that affects the brain chemistry and aids with sleep, they'd done sleep studies with people all wired while listening to whale songs. Maybe that was it — just get him some whale songs. If it worked however, he'd be done, and back in the pool. Peter knew he'd have to wing it.

Peter's eyes grew heavy and he let out a violent yawn. Yawning was a way for the brain to get more oxygen, Peter knew this. He also knew there was no oxygen here, not really, and his brain wasn't real either. Figuring it must be instinct rather than functional, Peter forgot about it and went to bed. At least, what he assumed to be the bed. It was a raised bit of rock that was somewhat flat. Lying down he noticed a kink in the bed around his lower back, probably designed that way, so he wouldn't be too comfortable. Perhaps he could raise it with Balthazar tomorrow, say something like, he couldn't work under these conditions. It would be bullshit however, could they tell? Did they have some power that detected lies? Would they even need one? Peter was never a good liar.

Peter realised he was spiralling, he cleared his mind of any thought and let his body go heavy, submitting to the rock below and falling into a deep, though unpeaceful, sleep.

11

Balthazar looked back at his bed as he was leaving, his latest conquest still sleeping soundly. He didn't normally trust anyone alone in his home, but this was a violent creature, and he was afraid to wake them. Of course, he would never admit this.

On his way to retrieve Peter, Balthazar felt a heavy weight on his shoulders. He was the right-hand man to the ultimate boss and here he was serving as manager to a fucking pianist. The worst of it was he knew this little project would never work. How could it? The boss would simply be enraged at yet another failure, and Balthazar was sure to bear the brunt of this ensuing fury. Peter was only human, it wasn't his fault, so Balthazar tried not to hold it against him, but still, what could he do? Besides anything else, he had perhaps been in the pool for too long. Maybe he has lost too much of himself?

Balthazar knew he would have to talk it over with the boss, he would have to persuade him to give this up, but he couldn't say it outright or, he'd be fired on the spot. Maybe the boss would be more open after meeting Peter, he's not a man that instils confidence after all.

The door was shut, and Balthazar thought about knocking, then he remembered he was a fucking demon and Peter was just a human, so he stormed through the door, shocking Peter awake, and dragged him outside.

"Jesus Christ, Balthazar, what the fuck!" Peter protested.

"Do us a favour, don't use that name in front of the boss." They were walking together now, after Peter had eventually composed himself. Balthazar could just teleport himself and Peter there in an instant, but he needed the walk this morning. Peter had managed to compose himself, but Balthazar hadn't yet, not that Peter could tell. Meeting Heather today will be insufferable, Balthazar was already certain. She would be cutting him a look, saying everything without a word, making him feel like shit for running ridiculous errands despite his supposed standing in the hierarchy. The worst part was how true it all was.

Heather was twiddling her thumbs when they arrived. Staring off into space, thinking about her former life. *Fucking humans*, Balthazar thought as they pulled up to her desk.

"So, is this the guy?" Heather asks as she snaps back to reality.

"Of course this is the guy. You *know* this is the guy. What a stupid fucking question," snapped Balthazar, he wasn't really angry at her, but she was an easy outlet for his frustration.

"I'm just being polite," Heather defended.

"Well, just don't. Look around you, where the fuck do you think you are? I'm not bringing you a sick ferret, I'm not asking you to remove the testicles of my prize pit bull, you're not a fucking a vet any more. Now stop fucking around and let him know we're here." Peter side-eyed Balthazar with a mix of shock and confusion, he didn't know this person, he didn't know what Balthazar had against her, she seemed perfectly nice to him.

Heather buzzed the intercom and notified the boss.

"He said to give him a minute or two," Heather informed Balthazar.

"Well, which is it, one minute or two?"

"He said exactly that, a minute or two, I wouldn't paraphrase him," Heather explained. "I'm Heather by the way, you must be Peter." Heather extended her hand and Peter accepted.

"Nice to... meet you." Peter's voice broke halfway through the sentence and he had to clear his throat to finish it. This was the first human he had met since getting here, at least he assumed she was human, based on Balthazar's outburst earlier.

"Seriously?" Balthazar scoffed.

"I assume we're going to be seeing a lot of each other, this will go a lot more smoothly if we're acquainted. That's what you want right? To spend as little time as possible out here?" Heather tried to keep a neutral face, to not scowl or raise an eyebrow, it was something she had mastered while explaining to rich white people why she knew better than their Facebook groups what was best for their pets.

"Fair enough," Balthazar conceded. They all looked around awkwardly for a few more moments before the intercom buzzed again.

"You can go right ahead," Heather said. Peter looked confused again as the intercom was just an inaudible noise to him.

"Thank you very much." Balthazar bowed sarcastically, before leading Peter into the office. Peter felt his chest tighten. He was about to meet Satan.

"Sir?" Balthazar said as he tentatively opened the door.

"Yes, come in," the boss replied, and they entered.

"Good morning sir, this is Peter, the musician." Balthazar motioned to Peter like he was a museum attraction.

"Yes, very good, could you leave us now Balthazar?" The boss had yet to acknowledge Peter, he hadn't even looked at him yet. Balthazar was confused, he hadn't expected this, and he didn't like it.

"Excuse me sir?" Balthazar said, visibly, and audibly, upset.

"Did I stutter? I will not repeat myself," the boss snarled.

"Yes, of course." Balthazar looked briefly at Peter, shooting him a look like he was parent dropping off their kid at someone else's house, warning them to behave. Then he left. Peter was now alone in a room in the deepest part of hell, with the ruler of the Underworld.

The devil looked straight at Peter for the first time. "Hello Peter."

12

Peter was frozen to the spot. He had always pictured the devil as a tall, bright-red skinned figure with a pointed tail and snake's tongue. Now, here stood before him a tall, bright-red skinned figure with a pointed tail and a snake's tongue. The logical part of his brain kicked in and he realised this was simply the filter doing its work and presenting the devil in a way that made sense to him.

"Please, take a seat." The devil gestured towards a small wooden chair at the other side of his desk. After a slight pause, where Peter considered why he was being so polite, he walked over and sat down. Only once Peter was seated did the devil walk behind his desk and take his seat on his throne. "Now, I'm aware Balthazar has filled you in on the details, however, I thought we should have a little chat first, just to make sure we're all on the same page, as it were."

"Yes, of course." Peter was sweating now, or at least he would be, if that were possible. He shifted uncomfortably in the chair, which wasn't comfortable, "Um… what do I call you?" The devil, who had been looking around his desk and fiddling with stuff, stopped and looked right at Peter.

Peter held the gaze, fully realising, for the first time, that he was staring right into the eye of the literal antichrist. The devil seemed to be calculating, but then he relaxed.

"Well, technically you're working for me. So, how about we simplify things, and you can just call me 'boss'." The devil sat back on his throne, satisfied with this resolution.

"OK, cool, got it boss." The devil raised his eyebrow slightly, very slightly, Peter never saw it move, but he could tell by the judging expression now resting on his face.

"Indeed. OK, what I want you to do is to explain to me, in your words, why you think you're here." Peter was stunned, he had not expected to be put on the spot like this.

"OK… sure… yes…" he stammered, and as he did so, he began to shrink till he was almost having to stretch up to peer over the top of the desk. "Well, you're having some… issues, which is like, that's fine you know, everybody does, I'm sure. So… you want me to… uh… write some music, to try and… uh… help you out," Peter finished and looked into the devil's face to see if this was satisfactory, but he gave nothing away.

"And do you think it's possible?" the devil asked. Peter really wasn't expecting that question, he tried not to pause but he wasn't sure if he got away with it.

"Of course I do, boss." Peter grew a little larger as he tried to project as much confidence into this answer as possible. It would only occur to him later that perhaps the devil had not wanted this answer, perhaps he wanted him to be honest.

"All right then, what's the first step?" Peter was, yet again, surprised. It hadn't occurred to him that he would be in charge, he presumed he would just be told what to do. The devil looked him up and down as he thought. Peter didn't like the inspection that his eyes were giving him, but he had to think about this, he couldn't just spit out any old answer. He finally came up with something, but he couldn't help his mind wandering. Would he be able to stay just one step ahead? Surely he would have to come up with a longer term plan, an endgame of sorts. Peter snapped back to the present.

"I should get to know you a little better, so I can tailor the music to you. So, we should have a longer conversation, where I can take some notes." The devil narrowed his already narrow eyes, Peter could tell he didn't like this answer, he obviously didn't want some human prying into his personal business. After a time though, he sighed heavily and said,

"OK, we'll set that up." Peter was amazed, he must be desperate. Maybe he had more leverage than he first thought. Maybe he was in full control here. Peter considered doubling down and demanding some things while he felt he still had the upper hand, but he decided not to overplay it just yet. *Patience,* he thought to himself. *Patience.* The devil leaned forward and took Peter in as he was thinking. *Oh shit,* thought Peter. *Does he know what I'm thinking? Is that a power of his?* He tried to take some cool, calming breaths to try and not give anything away, he didn't think it was working. Eventually, the devil backed up in his throne.

"You can see yourself out. Speak with Heather and she'll tell you what to do now, and if Balthazar is still out there can you tell him to come in." Peter was stuck to the chair, he had to concentrate awfully hard to prise himself out of the small, uncomfortable, wooden chair.

"Yes… boss." Peter forced his legs to move and he left the office, feeling like he may collapse at any given moment.

After finally getting outside, Peter allowed himself a moment of weakness, putting his hands on his knees and breathing heavily. Glancing to his side, he could see Balthazar at Heather's desk, they were both looking at him now. They were not judging him as he had expected, the look on their faces was one of recognition and understanding. Clearly this was a common reaction to meeting the devil. Balthazar came over and put a hand on his back.

"OK, stand up straight, come on now." Peter did so and Balthazar smiled at him, and for the first time, it was genuine, it wasn't cutting or mocking. Perhaps now they had some common ground.

"He… the boss wants to see you." Balthazar looked a little confused at Peter's message, or more likely he was confused at how he delivered it. Either way, he didn't question it, and went into the devil's office. Peter meandered over to Heather's desk, like a baby deer learning to walk.

"Hi, uh, I'm supposed to arrange something, to come back?" he stammered. Heather looked left and right, carefully peering as if she could see around corners. Finally, she came back to Peter.

"We should talk. Come with me." Heather stood up and walked off. Peter instinctively looked back at the devil's office, like a child looks out for a parent before doing something they know is wrong and likely to land them in trouble. He wasn't given time to think too much, as Heather had almost disappeared by the time he looked back, he followed, confused and more than a little scared.

13

Balthazar closed the door behind him and took a seat at the desk where the devil was still seated at his throne. The small wooden chair had gone and had been replaced by something much more suited to Balthazar's position as right-hand man.

"So, how did it go?" Balthazar rarely spoke first in this office, but he was impatient, of the music thing but also the whole ordeal in general, it had worn him down.

"Well, he lied to my face, so at least he has some balls. I guess I have *you* to thank for that. He doesn't think it'll work." The devil admitted.

"I see." Balthazar tried not to look happy about this, but he had 'I told you so', written all over his face.

"Yes, I can see that you're devastated," the devil said sarcastically. "It doesn't mean it isn't possible. In fact, I see this as a positive," the devil said unconvincingly.

"How so?"

"You know what humans are like, they're notoriously unconfident. There're very few cocky ones that can actually back it up. Most of the time, the real talents are humble," the devil explained, although Balthazar suspected he was speaking to himself more than to Balthazar.

"That's a good point sir, how would you like me to proceed?" Balthazar asked. The devil thought a good deal about this before responding.

"Speak to the human, make sure he understands what's at stake here. He wishes to speak to me, one-to-one, to try and 'tailor the music' or some such bullshit. I believe he's stalling, still believing that there's a way out for him. I need him to know his fate is sealed. We can't have him wandering around thinking he can get away with anything. He has to go to work," the devil punctuated this final point by leaning forward and loudly tapping the desk with his finger.

"Understood, sir," Balthazar conceded, but the devil was not impressed with his attitude.

"I respect that you don't agree with this and I respect you, Balthazar. But you don't understand. You don't understand what I'm going through. You don't need to agree with me, just do as you're told, without the fucking attitude, or I'll find someone who will." The devil and Balthazar stared off for a few seconds. Balthazar broke first.

"Of course, sir. I apologise. I'll speak to him right away," Balthazar responded. The devil was satisfied, primarily with his own management style; something that was held against him when he first applied for the job.

"Do it quickly, Heather is probably in his ear already."

“What does she know?” Balthazar asked, wide-eyed at this remark. The devil waved off his concerns.

“Nothing she can say, she’s bound not to say anything that can interfere, even if she wanted to, she couldn’t.”

“Right.” Balthazar exhaled, relieved. He then left before being asked to. The boss was right apparently, as both Heather and Peter were nowhere to be found. They would be easy to find but Balthazar decided to let them chat. Heather couldn’t tell him anything meaningful, she could only confuse or scare him, and he was already both of those things. Balthazar decided to take the rest of the morning off, he had been working overtime with Peter for most of the night. The boss was starting to annoy him, he’d been chewed out more times than he could count in his long life, but this time was different. This time, he hadn’t fucked up in any meaningful way, he wasn’t to blame for anything. The boss was just pulling rank, and he never pulled rank. Balthazar sulked all the way to his home, feeling smaller than he had in a long, long time.

14

Peter had followed Heather into a meeting room of sorts, or at least the Underworld equivalent. There was a stone table surrounded by seats and what looked like a floating screen at one end of the room. Heather snapped her fingers in his face to get his attention, as his eyes were wandering around.

"The room isn't important; we probably don't have a lot of time." Heather tried to get across the seriousness of the situation as quickly as possible but Peter, buoyed by his earlier negotiation skills, failed to grasp that he was in any real danger.

"Sure, yeah, what's up?"

"What's up? Do you know where the fuck you are?" Heather wasn't really asking so she didn't wait for an answer, even though Peter was opening his mouth to give one. "They're not telling you the truth, at least not all of it. How long did they say you had been under?"

"Under? You mean the pool thing?"

"Yes, whatever you call it."

"A few months."

"OK, well that's… that's… dammit." Heather cursed herself, of course this would happen. Peter was simply confused, a prevailing mood for him since this whole shit started.

"What's wrong?"

"OK, I can't tell you."

"Because it's too dangerous?" Peter enquired.

"No, I physically can't tell you, it's like… magic or something, you're in hell remember?" Heather explained, more than a little annoyed at his naivety.

"Sure, sure, of course, sorry." Peter still wasn't getting how serious this was. "So, you can't tell me what's really going on, but I'm guessing I've been down here a little longer, just based off what you're saying?" Peter looked to Heather for some form of non-verbal confirmation, but it wasn't forthcoming, "I'm guessing you can't gesture the truth. OK, whatever. Well, I feel pretty good you know, like, I haven't 'faded away' all that much or anything so it can't have been too much longer than that." Heather's entire body tensed up; she was desperate to give him some kind of hint, but that bastard wouldn't let her.

"I really can't say," she said, exhausted.

"Fair enough, well let me ask you something else then, unrelated. How long have you been here? Like, out here, alive," Peter asked, thinking about what he could arrange for himself.

"I'm not alive, for fuck's sake, and neither are you. It's hard to tell how long, but it's been a few years at least."

“Interesting… interesting.” Peter stroked his chin, completely ignoring the first part of her answer. Heather looked at his oblivious, little face and could see his mind considering all sorts of possible ‘lives’ for himself. She conceded that she couldn’t help him, he would find out for himself soon enough.

“You know what, you seem to be in control of the situation, forget I said anything,” Heather said. She didn’t even try to conceal her sarcasm, but Peter’s arrogance allowed him to completely miss it.

“Okay, thanks anyway.” Peter gave her a condescending smile and patted her shoulder. Heather looked at his hand in utter disdain, but of course, he didn’t notice that either.

“We should go back, Balthazar is probably looking for you, or not… he’s been a bit off lately. Why don’t you just go back to your room. I’ll give you a call when the boss wants to see you next.”

“Sounds good.” They left the room, Heather directed Peter to his temporary home and then she went back to her desk. *Poor guy,* she thought. *He had no idea that the lies they had told him extended beyond the time he was brought out the pool.* Heather’s sympathy faded as she replayed the conversation they just had in her head. She was trying to help and he couldn’t see it. Not because he was confused or scared, but because he was arrogant enough to believe he could figure something out on his own. He honestly believed he had some control over his destiny in this place.

Prick, she finally thought to herself as some low-level minion approached her desk looking to see the boss. *Bad fucking timing buddy*, she thought, as she buzzed the big man.

15

Balthazar was three drinks deep before he fully realised he hadn't made it home. His legs had taken over as he entered a fugue state and they had dragged him to his happy place. Well, ordinarily it was a happy place. All the usual demons were here, drinking, singing, debauching; it was dark, dank and damp, with a sorrowful air that seemed to be blowing through the vents. Normally, he was certain heaven couldn't have been much better than this place. But something was off this time.

Balthazar was standing at the bar thinking about Peter when a large, clammy hand slapped his shoulder from behind.

"Hi there, Zar!" He turned, startled, to see Tantalus drawing up a stool next to him. *Not this cunt*, Balthazar thought.

"Don't call me that, Tantalus," responded Balthazar, sternly. How he would have loved to choke him out just for dreaming of using that nickname, but he knew he couldn't. While not as high-ranking as Balthazar, Tantalus worked a crucial job here, and he did it better than anyone else before him. Balthazar long suspected there was some foul play but without any evidence he couldn't go around making accusations. He thought about it once, but eventually decided that being a slimy cunt wasn't sufficient evidence.

"Sorry, Balthazar, an honest mistake." Tantalus had enough sense not to provoke him too much, despite his untouchable status granted by his position. "Drink?"

"Sure, thanks." Balthazar side-eyed Tantalus, he was usually the last one to offer. This was highly suspicious behaviour. But Balthazar didn't concern himself too heavily; while Tantalus prided himself on being sneaky and subtle, the truth was he was extremely transparent. He would reveal himself soon enough.

The drinks arrived and they toasted to all the damned souls, as was usually appropriate. They both took a large sip and then Tantalus leaned in a little closer, peering over his shoulder as he did so. Balthazar looked down at the top of his head, he was much shorter than he, and was always hunched over. He looked like a gothic gargoyle, to go with his sneaky, cunt-ish demeanour.

"Listen, Balthazar, I've been hearing some rumblings."

"You should get that checked out, might be something in the ears," Balthazar joked. He had no wish to get into this with anyone, never mind Tantalus.

"You know what I mean, there's a new human around," Tantalus pried further.

"Nothing strange about that, we pull humans up all the time for various odd jobs." Balthazar did his best to play it off as nothing, even though it wasn't.

"This one's different, he's here for the boss. It's all very hush-hush."

"Then maybe you should fucking *hush*." Balthazar turned to Tantalus for the first time and stared him down. He immediately cursed himself, that was exactly what Tantalus was looking for. Knowing Balthazar would never tell him exactly what he was doing he just needed a reaction to confirm his suspicions.

"I see," Tantalus hissed.

"Tantalus, some friendly advice, leave this alone."

"Leave what alone? Like you say, there's nothing to it." Tantalus smirked, finished his drink and skulked away.

Balthazar cursed his stupidity again, he couldn't blame the drink, he was a seasoned drinker after all. Tantalus had an eidetic memory. If he went through his internal files of all the souls he had captured, he could narrow it down to a handful of candidates. This was potentially quite dangerous, not just for Balthazar but for the boss himself. Tantalus may have eyes on the top job, and he was well liked in certain circles for his work on bringing in souls.

For the time being it was the least of his worries, Balthazar put a pin in it and ordered another drink. *One thing a fucking time,* he thought. *And at this time, zero things.* He closed his eyes and inhaled deeply, allowing all his worries to wash over his mind.

He should find Peter and sort him out; he should apologise to Heather, her situation wasn't her fault; he should have an intervention with the boss; he should throttle Tantalus against a wall and ram a fist through his fucking skull like drywall. He should get some rest. *We all need some rest*, he said to himself, so he left, meandering home.

16

Peter sat on the piano stool, facing sideways to it and staring at the wall. He was trying to scheme, but he wasn't a schemer. It was part of the reason he never got anywhere when he was alive, he liked to blame bad luck, and Karen, but the truth is he never had any plans. It wasn't his strength, he just assumed that good stuff would happen to him if he kept working and kept playing, but he never went out and made things happen for himself. Now he had no choice.

Peter saw a lot of ways out; he just wasn't sure what 'out' meant. Maybe he could even get to heaven, if such a place even existed, it had just occurred to him that he didn't know for sure. *It has to*, he thought. *No yin without yang after all.* His primary focus was on staying out of the pool, however. Heather had managed for years, perhaps he could carve out some kind of role like hers, playing piano for the devil on a full-time basis, his own personal virtuoso, till the place freezes over. Anything had to be better than fading away, surely. Was continuing to exist enough? Was that a life?

Peter mused for a while about the irony of it all. When he was alive, he wasn't concerned much with living. Now he was dead, it was all he cared about. It made him laugh, something he hadn't done for a while, even when he was still alive.

Back to the here and now, Peter has to come up with a line of questions for the devil. They had to be insightful but not too invasive, substantial but not saturated, and most importantly, not complete bollocks. Peter wished he had a pen and paper to take notes. Looking at the piano he suddenly noticed a pad and pen had appeared. *Interesting,* he thought. Peter looked back towards the wall and wished for a fleshlight. Looking back at the piano, the pad and pen sat by themselves. Peter was disappointed, his newfound powers seem limited, perhaps they only pertained to things that may help the devil.

Although maybe it was a sin thing? Maybe as a human you were forbidden to do 'impure' things in the ethereal plane. Would you be able to masturbate in heaven? That would be weird though; sinful on Earth but anything goes in heaven. It would be hell if you couldn't though. What about anal? Peter never liked that in any case. Was hell the only place you could have fun? Clearly not, or the fleshlight would have appeared. Why was his first thought about masturbation anyway? Peter had been alone for so many years that he couldn't wish for a beautiful woman, just a tool for self-pleasure, the only kind he got towards the end of his life.

Peter pulled himself out of the rabbit hole and shook his head to clear the thoughts, impure or otherwise. He grabbed the pad and pen and began scribbling away. It was all nonsense, but it was good nonsense, sensible nonsense. Looking at the first few notes he had written; Peter was strangely proud of himself. This may just work. Instinctively Peter turned to the piano and started doing some warm-up exercises, to get the dexterity going. Procrastination was always Peter's first choice whenever things were starting to go well.

Just as he was starting to enjoy himself there was a bright spark in his head, like a hot flash of light. It startled him so much he fell off the stool. Peter assumed this was what Heather meant when she said she would call him but then Balthazar came through the door.

"Hey, thought I'd knock first, in case you were rubbing one out. What are you doing on the floor?" Balthazar said as he strode into the room.

"Wait, I *can* do that?" Peter said, remembering his previous musings.

"Ah Peter, we've still a lot to talk about." Balthazar looked down at Peter on the floor and outstretched his hand to help him up. Peter looked up at the hand for a while as though wary of it, as if something terrible would happen just by making contact with it. Taking the chance, Peter reached out and Balthazar pulled him to his feet. Nothing bad happened.

17

Peter and Karen were sat in the back of a taxi, as far apart from each other as was physically possible within the confines of the vehicle. They were trundling home from the latest label to reject Peter; he sat forlorn on one side while Karen sat furious on the other.

"You don't know how to sell yourself. It's a marketplace, you can't just 'let the music do the talking'. You idiot," she had told him earlier, as they were waiting for the taxi.

"I thought I had it. You should have seen their faces when I was playing," Peter had pleaded with her, but she had heard it before.

"They don't care about how good you are, you know how many fucking people have talent? It takes more than talent Peter, if you haven't figured that out yet I don't think you ever will."

"You weren't in the room Karen, if you could've seen them—"

"Just shut the fuck up Peter."

The taxi pulled up at the block of flats and Karen paid. Peter walked ahead of Karen, sulking. He felt like a child that had been sent home from school and was being marched into the house by their furious mother. Peter half-expected to be told to go to his room as soon as they walked through the door. A much worse fate awaited Peter, however.

Karen closed the door gently, as Peter placed his bag down in the hallway and hung up his jacket. Looking back over his shoulder, Peter noticed Karen still had her hand on the door, hunched and breathing slowly.

"Karen?" He was concerned, but not for her. She didn't move, but she did finally speak.

"I need you to leave, Peter."

He stood motionless; he was unsure what to do with his hands. Putting them in his pockets would be too casual, folding his arms will make him look angry and putting them on his hips would just be weird given the circumstance. So, they hung lifeless by his side.

"Leave? What do you mean *leave*?" he asked. Now Karen turned, fury and disappointment etched on her face.

"Leave Peter! I mean get out. Get out of my house, get out of my fucking life, you worthless piece of shit." Peter was marginally taller than Karen, but in her heels, she looked down on him, in life she looked down on him, now more than ever she looked down on her supposed meal ticket with disgust. Peter felt it all.

A week later he was lying on his cousin's couch. This was not his first rodeo and he had developed a non-verbal agreement. Peter knocks on the door, bag in hand, and is welcomed without a word. The waiting was a drag and

Peter felt a heavy weight on his chest. Karen would call, she wouldn't apologise, she wouldn't ask him to come back, she wouldn't cry or show any real emotion at all. Peter would be summoned back with a single word, 'OK'. He would pick up the phone, and after a deafening silence she would utter the magic word and he would skulk home.

Before then, it was just a lot of waiting around, watching TV, and trying not to get in his cousin's way. Peter was left pondering. Years wasted with Karen, each more painful than the last, exacerbated by every failure and missed opportunity he had along the way. He should get out, but Lord knows he can't afford his own place. The inconvenient truth was that Peter was stuck. Stuck in a marriage, stuck with his career, stuck in life, going through a cycle of depression, waiting and hoping for a change that would never come.

Peter had thought about suicide, but he wasn't suicidal. Just to pass the time he would think about how he would do it. He didn't have the balls to pull a trigger, and where would he get a gun anyway? This wasn't the US. Jumping off a building or a bridge seemed the easiest way but what if he had doubts while halfway down? What if he survived the fall? Then there was hanging, which just seemed so... dramatic. That wasn't Peter's style.

Of course he would never try anything. But it comforted to him to think about it. This was how he spent his days on his cousin's couch; waiting for his wife, whom he hated, to let him back into the house that his parents-in-law paid for, to be allowed back into his bedroom which she designed, into the bed she picked out. Peter couldn't help but feel like an interchangeable piece in her life. If it wasn't him it would be some other arsehole and nothing would change. He had no effect on Karen's world, it would look exactly the same without him. *But what the fuck else am I supposed to do,* he thought.

18

Tantalus watched it all. Not live, of course, but on a replay in his own mind. He watched Karen kick him out once again. He watched all her eye-rolls and heavy sighs. He watched Peter play his piano, and he was good. He watched his spirit fade, his head lower and the dark thoughts circle him. *Yes,* thought Tantalus. *This is the guy right here. This is the poor fucker right here.* Tantalus remembered him well, he remembered how easy it was to convince Karen, how little work he had to do. It was the first time in his storied career he felt a modicum of sympathy for the soul he was dragging to hell. It didn't last long, that feeling, but it did surprise him. Nonetheless, this was the fucker right here. Tantalus had to be careful, now was not the time to be rash, caution was required. What lay ahead would be delicate, yet brutal. Still, he couldn't hide his glee. Time to do what he does best, time to whisper in some ears.

There were only a handful of high-ranking demons assembled in the room, all looking at each other, wondering why they would be called together, considering each other's position and what it could all mean. Tantalus revelled in the anticipation.

"Sires," he said. The demons all turned to the head of the room, they had barely noticed that Tantalus was in the room, he had their full attention with that single word and teasing smile, as he continued, "He's weak." Tantalus let the statement work its way through the room. They were all slightly puzzled, a few began muttering to each other. But one, one understood fully. Tantalus locked eyes with her, Peri. Peri was long underrated in the Underworld mainly due to her quiet, unassuming nature. She had the moniker of demon like everyone else in the room, but Tantalus knew she was a fucking god, as sure as he knew that the river Styx flowed and fire reigned.

"He's always been weak, I assume you mean his position has weakened?" Peri asked, silencing the rest in the room. She sat nearest to the front, Tantalus had ensured that, they all looked forward to her, but she never looked back, she never looked away from Tantalus. Some were disgusted, how dare she speak without addressing them? Tantalus felt this but ignored them all.

"Yes, of course. I have information. I can't reveal exactly what that is right now, but trust me—"

"Trust you? Seriously?" Someone shouted. Tantalus didn't even look up at his interrupter, he couldn't tell who it was but it didn't really matter, most were here to make up the numbers.

"Yes. We, all of us, have been stuck in the doldrums for centuries through his leadership. Never moving up, never going anywhere. If you want that to change that then you'll have to trust me." Tantalus did look up now. "Of course, you can always leave." He motioned to the door. The demon who interrupted thought for a long moment, looking up and down the line of the other would-be dissenters. Then he left. *Great*, thought Tantalus. *Now I'll have to kill him*. And he had rather hoped to avoid any of that.

"Follow me, and we'll rule this place. Every major position, every major power will go to the people in this room."

"Follow you?" Peri asked, she wasn't really questioning, just teasing, and Tantalus fucking loved it. Peri laid a genuine claim to the throne, but she knew as well as he did, she didn't have the reputation to lead this operation with any chance of success.

"You're talking about a coup? An insurrection?" Another demon had piped up.

"No, of course not. This isn't like the old days; we don't need to march up the hill in arms. Once this information gets out, and I'll make sure of that, the throne will be vacant. All we need to do is be ready with a platform, we make the best possible case to take over before anyone else even has a chance to think about it. We drum up support before it happens and then we can't lose." Their body language was changing, they had gone from uncomfortable and perplexed to agreeing and excited. They saw the possibilities, and there was a murmur of agreement. Tantalus looked again to Peri, she was beaming at him, she had never looked at him like this before. He continued with more confidence than he had ever felt, her gaze empowering him beyond what he thought possible. "Those in favour say 'Aye', and I'll be in touch later with further instruction." They all looked at each other, except Peri, who never looked away from Tantalus.

"Aye!" The said in unison.

"Aye," repeated Peri, softer, just for Tantalus to hear.

After everyone else had left, Peri stayed behind. They were both sitting now, across from each other, Peri hadn't moved as the others left and she had invited Tantalus to sit without saying a word.

"Do you really need these idiots? You know you and me could do this ourselves," she stated.

"We need numbers, support, allies. The only *individual* I need is you. You've always had your eye on leadership and I know for a fact you know how to get there."

"No. I know what to do once I'm there. Apparently, *you* know how to get there."

"I do now." Tantalus was oozing swagger in a way he never had before. His reputation was a creepy hunchback, skulking around in the shadows. Peri made him stand tall.

"What makes you think I want to be your number two, or anyone's number two for that matter?"

"You could be number one but we both know you're not there yet," Tantalus explained. Peri had no wish to argue the point any further so, she changed track. "I'm not going to be your assistant, running around doing errands like fucking Balthazar."

"No, of course not. You can do whatever you want."

"Except lead."

"You know what I mean." Tantalus was beginning to tire of defending himself. Peri sighed in defeat.

"OK, I'm in… I'm yours."

It was music, sweet music to his wretched ears. *What an angel*, Tantalus thought, as she left. *What a fucking angel.*

19

"I had no idea I could drink here. Will I even get drunk?" Peter asked as Balthazar passed him a glass.

"Back again already?" The bartender said to Balthazar.

"How about you mind your fucking business and just serve the fucking drinks, yeah?" Balthazar snapped back, and the bartender walked away. Peter felt relieved that he wasn't the only one that Balthazar spoke to like this, but at the same time, Peter felt a little less special. Balthazar turned to Peter. "Look Peter, you can do whatever the fuck I let you do. Right now, I'm letting you have a drink. Is this starting to make sense?" Peter looked at the glass in front of him and took a big, refreshing gulp.

"I guess so. So, I can only have a wank if you let me? Like, a cuckold?"

"You're a perverted little freak you know that? I mean, just absolutely obsessed with your own penis." Balthazar had meant to shame Peter, but Peter was used to it now and he just smiled and shrugged.

"Can you blame me? Don't you have… you know?" Peter gestured broadly at Balthazar's crotch. Balthazar leered at him incensed, but he calmed himself.

"Yes, Peter, I have genitals, though their form is far too complex for you to understand. We have no concept of sex or gender as demons. We're all kind of one thing."

"Ah." Peter couldn't hide his surprise at this. He looked around the room as if the others in the place could help him understand. "So, how come most people around here are male? Or is that just how I'm seeing them?" Balthazar looked around the room also.

"That would be your misogyny shining through Peter," Balthazar joked. "Just kidding. You're likely just more comfortable around men so that's how you're mainly seeing people. Your brain wouldn't make everyone male so you will likely be viewing a few demons as female. But it'll be fairly random who that applies to."

"But what about sex, not male or female, I mean *sex*. You know, fucking," Peter asked.

"Yes Peter, I know what you mean," Balthazar sighed. "Let me put this as simply as possible. We can all fuck each other, and the mechanisms for that would blow your tiny, little mortal brain. So, how about we leave it at that," Balthazar concluded.

"Fair enough. Thank you for clearing that up." Peter smiled and raised his glass to Balthazar, who chuckled a little. Perhaps he was beginning to like Peter. Peter was certainly beginning to like him. For all his aggression, he did seem to care.

“Why are you helping me?” Peter asked, curiously.

“It’s simple Peter; the easier you find it down here, the easier your job is. The easier your job is, the easier my *life* is,” Balthazar explained. Peter already figured that Balthazar had some self-interest in his well-being, but it still hurt a little bit to hear it out loud.

“I see,” he replied, taking a further drink,

“So, I’m going to give you some rules,” Balthazar said, either ignoring or, not noticing, Peter’s slump in mood. “First off, don’t talk back to anyone down here. You might get away with it when you’re talking to me because I know who are. But humans are extremely expendable down here, and most of these guys love fucking with them.” Balthazar took a long drink, before continuing. “Second, don’t fuck around with the boss. Don’t stall while trying to think of a way out of here; there isn’t one, it doesn’t fucking exist. So, start taking this seriously, and get to fucking work.” Balthazar looked over his shoulder before his final point. “Lastly, if you meet a cunt called Tantalus, don’t say a fucking word, just ignore him, he can’t make you talk. In fact, he may not even tell you his real name, if you meet anyone that looks like a Tantalus, don’t say a fucking word.”

“I’ve never met anyone called Tantalus. I don’t know what they look like.”

“Trust me, you’ll know.”

“OK, sure.” They both sat in silence, drinking, while Peter took in all the information he had just been told. They must have known he was stalling and scheming. His spirits were now dampened by Balthazar's words. Perhaps it was time to accept his fate. Perhaps there was no way out. But that didn't mean there weren't options. Surely to God there were options?

"Who is this Tantalus guy anyway?" Peter asked, trying to take his mind off his inevitable fate.

"He's just a cunt, don't worry about him." Balthazar waved it off, but Peter could tell there was more to it than that. Balthazar thought a lot of people were cunts, but he only warned Peter about this one. Peter had enough on his plate, so he put Tantalus to the back of his mind. Besides, he was beginning to get a familiar buzz of the drink, it worked quickly, and he was feeling good.

"Good shit, right?" Balthazar asked, noticing Peter's intoxication.

"Eh... aye... it's no bad. No bad at all," Peter slurred, turning to Balthazar. They both smiled, and they continued drinking for a long time.

20

Peter noticed, truly noticed, for the first time, just how fucking *warm* it was down here. Not hot, not boiling, not intolerable, just a constant, unrelenting warmness. Enough to make you uncomfortable while still being able to endure. This feeling wasn't new to Peter, he had spent his whole life uncomfortably enduring. Even so, he shifted in his chair and fidgeted with his pen. All in stark contrast to the cool, stoic figure that sat across him.

The devil was growing impatient, but he never let on. He had the air of someone who knew they were in total control. The devil was aware that Peter had been scheming and that this initial 'consultation' was a stalling tactic. But what was more important was that Peter knew he knew. Peter held no cards; he couldn't win because he wasn't even playing. He simply had to make the best of the situation and try to garner some useful information.

"So, when did these problems start?"

"I'm sorry, are you my psychiatrist? Because I thought you played the fucking piano?" The devil wasn't angry. In fact he was amused. He delivered the sarcasm calmly and sat poised while Peter fumbled with his notes.

"Yes, of course, sorry… eh boss. Sorry boss. Let me just…" Peter looked at everything he had written on the first page and realised it was no good, so he flipped to the second. "OK, here we go… what kind of music do you like?" The devil was surprised by the question. He had never been asked it before. Come to think of it, he had never been asked anything like it. Peter had been looking down at his notes awaiting an answer, but it never came. He looked up in time to see the devil blink a few times and lose his poise for a moment. It was just a moment, but Peter noticed it.

"Well, I suppose that you think I enjoy classical music given how old I must be?"

"Yes actually, that was my first thought, but you've existed long before that right?"

"Yes. Indeed." The devil had managed to compose himself with that little deflection, and now he could answer the question truthfully. "If I had to put a genre on it, I would have to say… swing." Peter was surprised but he wasn't sure why. The devil could have said literally anything, and he would have been surprised. Except for maybe heavy metal.

"Swing. Great. No Christian rock then?" Peter looked up to see if the joke had landed but the devil simply rolled his eyes. Peter was actually buoyed by the devil's answer because he could play swing. It was a common request during his days playing in a wedding band. He was starting to get some inspiration. He went off script. "How do you feel when you listen to music?"

"I'm not sure I understand." The devil noticed Peter's uptick in mood, it made him curious, but also a little suspicious.

"Well, does it make you sad? Happy? Does it calm you?" The devil understood now, and he sat back in his throne while considering. Peter knew he was onto something here.

"It… empties my mind. I listen to it at the end of the day."

"So, to *unwind*?"

"I am never wound to begin with!" The devil snapped.

"Yes, of course, sorry boss." Peter scribbled some illegible notes on his pad. For the first time he believed this whole thing may actually work. "Have you always listened to it at the end of the day? Even before you were in charge?"

"No actually," The devil was answering quickly now, with less consideration. Perhaps his guard was down. "Before I was in charge, I would listen at all times of the day. Of course, that was a long time ago, we had our own music but there was still less variety around."

"I see." Peter began writing.

"You see what?" the devil challenged, perhaps realising he was revealing more than he had planned.

"Uh… I just meant… like, it's an expression. I think I understand is all," Peter stammered. The devil appeared content with this answer and relaxed a little.

"OK," said the devil, with more than a little sizzle in his tone. This went unnoticed by Peter, who decided to pry further.

"Do you dance to music?"

"Excuse me?" The devil couldn't decide whether to be angry or confused.

"When music is playing—" Peter began but didn't get the chance to finish.

"I understood the fucking question." The devil stared Peter down, but Peter didn't flinch. *Impressive*, thought the devil. *He should be shitting himself.* "No. I'm not a dancer."

"So, when you're listening to music, what are you doing? Working? Sitting? Lying down?"

"Usually sitting."

"Here?" Peter motioned at the throne.

"No, rarely here. Usually at home."

"Got it." It had never occurred to Peter that the devil didn't *live* here. He knew it was just an office but even so, he couldn't picture the devil with a house and a bedroom, maybe some nice curtains and a shag carpet. It all came across as too homely for the prince of darkness.

"Is there anything else?" The devil wasn't really asking, he wanted Peter to leave. He felt that he had said enough. But Peter was oblivious to these cues.

"Yes, boss. One more question," Peter insisted. The devil sighed, but he allowed it, one more couldn't hurt. After the devil's nod, Peter continued.

"Have you already tried music to help you sleep?"

"Of course, I have, it didn't work. The music wasn't made for that, why the fuck do you think you're here?" the devil yelled. The sheer stupidity of the question annoyed him and further proved just how inferior humans are.

"Sorry boss. I figured; I was just wondering what didn't work about it? How did you feel when you tried it?"

"I felt exhausted, like I usually do, no change, no nothing. Are we about done here now?" The devil was now beckoning for Peter to leave with his hand. Finally taking the hint, Peter stopped scribbling and got up to leave. "Peter, wait one second." Peter turned around before he got to the door.

"Yes boss?"

"I'll expect something from you, soon. Heather will let you know how soon. Now get to work."

"Yes boss." Peter turned to leave again, closing the door gently behind him. He breathed heavily once he was outside. In… and out, in… and out, he repeated to himself, his head spinning.

"Feeling faint?" It was Heather, who had taken notice of his display.

"Yes, a little."

"He has that effect on people."

"Aye, he does indeed." Peter walked over to her desk, "I'm supposed to come back with something, soon."

"Yes, I know." Heather always seems to know; they couldn't possibly have spoken since the time he left the office. How the fuck does that work? "Three days, you have exactly three days to come up with something."

"Well, that's not a lot of time."

"Patience is a virtue, we're more about vices down here," Heather said, smiling.

"Good one," Peter said, before thinking about the three days ahead. "Wait, there's no sun down here, I won't really know what day it is."

"Of course, hold on." Heather rummaged around in one of her drawers before emerging with what looked like a watch. "Here you go." Peter looked at the watch face, there were no numbers on it, no dials, no hands, just a blue, smoky hue covering the face.

"I don't understand, how does it work?"

"Not sure, to be honest, but anytime you look at it, it tells you what you need to know." Peter thought about it for a second. He wondered what day it was back on Earth, then he looked at the watch. It burned red for a second before returning to that neutral, smoky blue. Heather noticed and knew what he was trying.

"It doesn't tell you anything about up there."

"Ah, of course." Peter thought again, this time about how much of the three days he still had left. The watch glowed with a green circle. The circle wasn't whole though, there was a small blue section from where the twelve on a clock would be. Like a pie chart. The green must represent the three days, and blue is the time that's passed.

"Yeah, that's better," Heather said. Peter smiled to himself, smug that he was able to read to magic hell watch.

"Thank you, Heather. I can honestly say no one has helped me more down here."

"I wouldn't get used to it. Besides, I am just doing my job."

"Of course, well, thanks anyway." Heather nodded and turned her attention back to the papers on her desk. Peter walked away, and once he was round the corner, he looked at the watch again. Again, it glowed with the green circle, but the blue section had gotten bigger. It was still small, but it was perceptibly bigger. *How the fuck?* thought Peter. *I just fucking looked at it*. Time was an abstract concept, like most things down here. Peter realised he would have to let go of what he knew before. The rules were different here, and time was ticking away. He half-ran back to his room and went straight to his Piano.

21

Balthazar sat at his desk staring at the large stack of papers that had grown like a fungus. He had been too busy with the boss and Peter that he hadn't spent much time here and now he had a backlog of shit to get through. Looking around his meagre workspace and considering the tediousness of his daily duties, Balthazar couldn't help but wonder if there was more to it than this. At least humans could dream of better things. They had the luxury of mortality, believing in a greater purpose or predestined opportunities, with their dreams unsullied by endless time. Balthazar, however, *knew* there was nothing more for him. There was a certainty to his limits that he couldn't help but loathe. Perhaps he would be better off as an ignorant mortal. At least then he could dream.

A knock on his door awoke Balthazar from his pondering. His assistant poked his head through.

"A general for you, sir?"

"Yes, send him in then." Balthazar straightened up in his chair and attempted to adopt an air of seniority as the general came in and took a seat.

"What can I do for you?"

“We’ve got a problem, sir. One of my lieutenants, he wants a better living space,” The general reported. Balthazar sighed. This wasn’t a common occurrence, but it happened just often enough to annoy him. The solution was more than simple to him, yet he was always burdened with explaining it.

“And why is that a problem?” Balthazar questioned. The general shifted in his seat; he had not expected to be challenged.

“Well… uh… if everyone starts demanding—”

“How long have they been working in this position?”

“A few centuries now, sir.”

“And are they good at their job?”

“Yes sir, one of the best.”

“So, give him his fucking living space.” Balthazar decreed. The general was shocked.

“Sir, how can we expect—”

“How can we expect to get the best out of our employees when we give them so much? Won’t they become complacent? Won’t they lose motivation?” Balthazar had heard it all before and it bored him. “If you want to keep people motivated and working you have to keep them happy. Part of that is giving them what they deserve. Even some humans have figured that one out by now. Are you stupider than *humans*?” Balthazar challenged. The general shot up in his chair.

“No! Of course not, sir,” the general answered quickly. Balthazar smirked, that one always worked. Every demon down here considered themselves far superior to all humans, but the truth was they were just as dumb. Just as easy to manipulate and control.

"Very well then. Give the demon his dues."

"Yes sir." The general left quickly, glad to escape without having to defend himself any further.

Balthazar turned his attention to the stack of papers. Reaching out a weary hand he picked the top of the pile and got to work. After a while, Balthazar got into a rhythm. Yes, it was tedious, but there is a meditative and therapeutic nature to the mundane. Just as he was starting to get through a fair stack of work, he got the call. That all too familiar red blaze fired up in his head.

"Fucking typical," Balthazar said to the empty room. He took a few moments to compose himself before appearing at Heather's desk.

"Good afternoon, Balthazar."

"The boss called me," Balthazar said without acknowledging Heather's greeting. He was in no mood to get into it with her.

"Yes, he'll just be a minute, you don't normally arrive so quickly so he's not quite ready," Heather stated this as a fact, but Balthazar invented undertones and took offense.

"What the fuck are you trying to say exactly?" he said, annoyed. Heather was genuinely surprised. She hadn't meant anything by it.

"Sorry Balthazar, I didn't mean anything," she explained.

"Yeah, OK." Balthazar back off and softened a little.

Heather looked at Balthazar, she didn't want to say anything, she knew she shouldn't, but the urge was too great. "Balthazar. Are you really OK with this whole thing? With Peter?" Balthazar looked at Heather. She never questioned him before.

"Why should I give a fuck? I don't give a fuck about you, do I?"

"Yes, but you never did to me what you did to Peter."

"Careful Heather, the boss likes you, but you are still replaceable." Balthazar was starting to get annoyed with the third degree. He knew that would be enough to shut her up for the time being. She didn't take it any further, but she didn't believe the apathetic, tough demon act.

"The boss is ready for you now," she said with a smile.

"Thank you." Balthazar bowed sarcastically, and went into the office. The devil was already sitting at his throne, calmly looking at the wall. It had been a while since Balthazar had seen him this calm. The last few times he had been summoned, the devil had been nothing short of frantic.

"This won't take long Zar, but feel free to take a seat."

"How did it go with Peter?" Balthazar asked, sitting across from the devil.

"Not too bad actually. It had started out as bullshit as we had expected, but I think he may actually be on to something," the devil explained. Balthazar was amazed.

"That's... great."

"I'm still not holding out much hope and I still want you to keep a firm eye on him."

"Yes, of course." Balthazar would have to talk to Peter again, the boss wouldn't give much away, and he had to know what happened today.

"There's another thing Zar. We can't have anyone finding out about this. Especially not what we did with Peter when we brought him out. That kind of information could ruin me, and by extension, you." Balthazar immediately thought of Tantalus. He pictured himself wringing the little cunt's neck and it brought him some peace. The boss was correct though; whilst Tantalus probably knew about Peter by now, he didn't know the whole story. That could be enough to protect them.

"I understand boss. I'll keep my ear to the ground and shut down any rumours." Balthazar considered telling the boss about Tantalus, but he figured it wouldn't do any good. It would simply cause some undue stress.

"Good, thank you Zar." Balthazar winced again at the use of his nickname. Fortunately, the boss never noticed.

Balthazar decided to go the long way back to his desk. His position had been safe for so long he never had to contend with the idea that it may be in jeopardy. He cursed himself for not considering this before and protesting harder against the whole plan. It was too late now, take it as it comes he told himself. Most considered him an easy target. It had been millennia since he had to fight for anything, but Balthazar knew he was still a warrior. He'll fight tooth and nail, and he wasn't afraid to fight dirty. He thought of Tantalus again. *Bring it on you bastard,* he thought to himself. The idea of a fight energised Balthazar, it got his juices flowing. His walk turned into a swagger as he meandered through the fire and brimstone.

22

Peter began piano lessons at age five. His mum had decided early on in his life that his intelligence would take him nowhere. Their solution was for him to learn a skill. Peter had often wondered if he would have been better off learning something practical, like woodwork or engineering, given the difficulty of finding work as a musician. But perhaps that would have been tantamount to child labour given his infancy.

His teacher was a stern, unforgiving German woman called Frieda. Peter was unable grasp the idea of association at five years old, and he grew up believing all German people to be mean. This lasted until an age that Peter is too ashamed to admit. She carried a cane which she would slam on the piano whenever he made a mistake. Every time she did so, it made Peter flinch. She never struck Peter with it but with every snap of the cane he believed she could. The threat was real. And so were the lasting effects. Throughout his childhood, he couldn't play piano without flinching every time he made a mistake, even when Frieda wasn't there.

Despite it all, his playing greatly improved. As his hands grew and he could reach the right keys without having to strain his fingers. Even the poker-faced Frieda couldn't help but flash a smile as Peter played. The piano became his identity. At school, he was known as 'the piano guy'. His schoolmates knew little about him, but they knew he was good at the piano. His parents would often introduce him to their friends by saying, 'This is our son Peter, he's good at the piano'. Through it all Peter forgot to develop a personality.

Peter remembered all this as he sat in his room in the depths of hell, gently running his finger along the keys of this new piano. He could faintly hear the crack of his teacher's cane, its echo reverberating off all the rocks and ringing in his ears. The music sheet in front of him was complete, and he was proud. For the last six months of his life, he had never looked up and seen a complete music sheet. A nervous excitement was brewing in the pit of his stomach. A feeling he knew so well in those early days. From those first few weeks of lessons, when he finally got a chord right, to rehearsing in his friend's basement and nailing a solo. It's a feeling that had become alien to him later in life and now, he distrusted it. It started to make him anxious. He had yet to play the lullaby as a whole and he didn't want to. He didn't want to ruin the moment, the feeling, the expectation was enough for him. Peter had experienced enough bitter disappointment in his life, he wasn't sure he could bear any more now that he was dead.

The watch that Heather had given him glowed on his wrist as his mind drifted to how much time he had left. Glancing at it, Peter could see the circle was almost entirely blue, with a tiny green sliver. He didn't have time to start again. This, right here in front of him, this was it. This *had* to be it. Yet, he still couldn't play. His fingers were locked, rigid, unmoving. Peter was good at the piano. He had always been good at the piano. But he had never been good enough. The pride he had felt moments before had evaporated and were replace by apprehension. His feelings of inadequacy kept him paralysed.

A sharp knock on his door made Peter jump. For a second, he thought his old teacher had returned and was banging on the door with her cane, demanding he play better. Peter gathered himself as Balthazar entered the room.

"Hello, Peter," he said, strolling to the piano and resting his arm on its body.

"Hello, Balthazar."

"You don't have much time left, and I know you know that," Balthazar said, gesturing to his watch.

"Yes… I… uh… I think I have something," Peter stammered.

"Said with the booming confidence that I've come to expect, Peter," Balthazar teased. Peter rolled his eyes at Balthazar's sarcasm.

"Well, I've never done this before."

"We'll take it slow. We'll be gentle and use plenty of lubricant."

“For fuck’s sake Balthazar.”

“What? I’m lightening the mood. C’mon then, play your… something.” Balthazar was gesturing now at the piano, waving Peter on like he was some kind of human jukebox. *I guess I am,* Peter thought.

“What… right now?” Peter couldn’t play the piece while he was alone, how could he possibly play in front of Balthazar? Balthazar leaned in close.

“Peter, if you can’t play for me, how do you expect to play for the boss?” It was a good point, and one that Peter had neglected to consider. Peter instinctively went into his preshow routine. He closed his eyes and straightened his back, breathing deeply. Keeping his eyes closed he tilted his head left, and then right, down, and then up. He locked his fingers together and pushed his palms away. Hearing that familiar crack of his knuckles awakened something in him. Opening his eyes Peter noticed Balthazar’s confused expression. He ignored him, put his fingers to the keys, and played.

It was beautiful. Peter’s fingers danced across the keys, delicate but decisive. The melody was better than he had imagined. It was his creation, and he was playing it. Yet, he was hearing it for the first time. Peter entered a trance, he floated above himself and watched this alien figure caress the piano and make it sing. Balthazar was amazed, he wasn’t sure what he was listening to, but he knew it was damn good. Peter finished with a flurry and looked up at Balthazar, ecstatic at his creation. Peter was good at the piano.

23

The flames danced and the rocks smouldered as Peri took a gentle stroll to the devil's office. She had no intention of speaking to the devil, she was after Heather. Peri mistrusted Tantalus; she knew he was at least somewhat enchanted by her but that would only go so far. Tantalus was known for backstabbing, he was a plotter, a schemer, a certified cunt. He was keeping information to himself and that gave him all the power. Peri wanted a piece of that, so she wanted to speak to Heather.

The devil had a bad habit of oversharing with his human underling. Maybe he trusted her, maybe he was careless. Whatever the case, it didn't matter. Peri knew that Heather wouldn't be able to tell her, she'd be physically incapable of saying the words. That was exactly the point, however. Peri would get the information she needed based on what she *didn't* say. It was a stupid loophole. One that was easily exploitable. One that wouldn't exist if she were in charge.

Heather saw her coming, she didn't see many strange demons, not at her desk anyways. This made her immediately suspicious, but she withheld judgement. This demon acted differently to the ones that normally graced her desk. Ordinarily, they were coy, shy, nervous. This demon strode down the hallway. Not arrogantly, in the fashion of Balthazar, it was a confident stride, slow but purposeful.

"Hello there," Peri said with a smile.

"Can I help you?" Heather asked.

"You most certainly can, Heather." Peri leaned on the desk, her smile growing.

"The boss is busy, and I don't think you have an appointment." Heather instinctively backed off in her chair as Peri leaned in. She made her uncomfortable.

"I don't. I'm not here to see him. I doubt he would see me anyway. You know what it's like with the mentality around here. It's much the same up top, am I right? Fucking leadership types." Heather eyed Peri with extreme suspicion. She hadn't expected a show of solidarity from an underling of the devil.

"I… I don't know what you're talking about." Heather chose her words carefully. She knew the punishment for dissent and it simply wasn't worth it to bond with this strange figure.

"Of course you don't, sweetheart," Peri said flippantly. This upset Heather. She had started off with 'fuck the patriarchy' and ended with 'sweetheart'. How very disappointing.

"Can I help you?" Heather repeated, still unsure about Peri's intentions.

"What do you know about a human called Peter?" Peri enquired. Heather was surprised she knew the name, and she couldn't hide her surprise either. Peri got exactly the response she was looking for. Tantalus hadn't told her much, but she had managed to entice that particular nugget of information from him. Now she had her 'in'.

"I don't know what you're talking about. Who are you exactly?" Heather replied, trying to turn the tables on Peri, but she wasn't even listening to her. Peri was *reading* her.

"I believe there was some, how do you say, dodgy business with his resurrection. Not just your standard soul collection from the pool, am I right?"

"Again, I don't know what you're talking about. I think I'm going to have to ask you to leave." It was too confrontational from Heather, too defensive.

"Oh, I won't be long, sweetheart. Was Balthazar responsible?" Heather said nothing this time. Maybe silence was how to deal with it. She had dealt with clients like this on a regular basis on Earth. Not just clients, but also colleagues, teachers, professors. Almost everyone she had met had ignored the words coming out of her mouth. At least on Earth she was normally in the right, she normally had her education and the truth on her side. Down here, in this moment, she was incapable of telling the truth. This demon was getting everything she wanted without Heather having to say a word, so she let her have it. Why give her the satisfaction of stumbling around for an answer.

"You clearly already know what you want to know." Heather rose from her seat unexpectedly, she even surprised herself. "Now if that's all, can you kindly leave? The boss is busy, which means I'm busy. So, I don't have time to deal with whatever bullshit this is." Heather pointed at the exit and stared Peri down.

"Very good, Heather. I'm proud of you, girl." Peri was impressed. This wasn't no sweetheart. "I'll leave you be. I apologise for my demeanour. It's nothing personal." Heather was still standing, still pointing. "I may have use for you yet, girl. Be seeing you." And with that, Peri left.

That must be bad news, thought Heather. She should tell the boss, but perhaps it wasn't worth worrying him about it. She could tell Balthazar, but she really, really, didn't like him. That was the only option though. Unless she didn't say anything. Why should she care anyway? She wasn't here by choice. It wasn't like she owed them anything. They had never told her exactly what it was that sent her down here in the first place. She had dedicated her to life to helping animals, she was nice to people, she even went to church. Not that she was a believer, but her mum was, and they always went together. Heather mulled all this over, as Balthazar appeared at her desk.

"Was that Peri? What did she want?" Balthazar barked.

"Hello to you too, Balthazar." Heather disappointed herself as she instinctively entered sarcasm mode.

"Yeah whatever, just answer the question."

“She never told me her name. She was asking about Peter, but I couldn’t tell her anything.”

“Does the boss know?”

“No. I don’t think so,” Heather answered, honestly. Balthazar looked down the hallway. This worried him. Tantalus was a scheming cunt, but he could deal with him. Peri was a different beast altogether; smart, confident, organised.

“OK, keep it that way.”

Peri sauntered her way home. Exactly as she had thought. Peter wouldn’t know, how could he? There was no point in telling him of course. What good would that do? There were places to go with this, however. This being hell, there weren’t many avenues for checks and balances, but a few did exist. Independent tribunals, courts that lived above bureaucracy, and factions that lived below it all. No doubt Tantalus planned to involve them all, but he was clumsy and careless. *I have to take charge,* she thought. She would have to keep him in check before he started gloating, more than likely to Balthazar. “*I have to take charge,*” she said to herself again. The flames danced a little quicker and the rocks smouldered with a little more sizzle as she made her way home. Peri would take charge. Peri would be *in charge*.

24

"So, do you have the recording?" The boss was in a good mood. Apparently even the devil was capable of optimism.

"Yep, poor bastard thought he had to perform live. I didn't tell him till I was leaving, it was too funny." Balthazar and the devil shared a good, hearty laugh. Balthazar hadn't realised how long it had been since they shared a laugh together. They were good friends before.

"Excellent. How was it?" The boss was eager, keen, excited. Balthazar shrugged.

"I don't really know music, boss. It seemed good to me. Peter was happy with it anyway."

"Yes, well, the human would be proud of his own work. That doesn't tell me much." The boss refused to use Peter's name. Balthazar couldn't tell if it was due to apathy or guilt. Although it was less likely to be the latter.

"All I can say is, I was pleasantly surprised, boss."

"Yes, good, good. I think I'll try it out this afternoon, a little power nap to get me through the day."

"Good idea, boss." Balthazar had reverted to his 'yes man' persona rather quickly today. He had planned to take Peter out to celebrate and was eager to leave. It only just occurred to him he would rather spend time with the human than his old friend. Had they morphed fully into employer-employee? Maybe if the poor fuck could get some rest, they could be friends again.

"So, what's going on out there? Anything I should be worried about?" The boss was searching through the papers on his desk, looking for anything of note. They hadn't spoken about work matters in weeks, and he hadn't expected to be asked directly.

"Uh... what do you mean, boss?" Balthazar asked, hesitantly. The devil stopped rifling through his papers and looked up at Balthazar, surprised.

"It's a pretty simple question Zar. I appreciate you holding the fort for me. Am just asking if there's anything I should know about," the devil clarified. Did he know? Did Heather say something? Was the boss testing him?

"Not off the top of my head, boss. Just the usual bullshit."

"Hmm. That's surprising."

"It is?" Balthazar was confused and worried.

"Yes. The word must be out on the human. No one will know why we brought him out, not even Heather is fully aware. But the circumstances in which we did it. I had expected someone to be raising questions," the devil responded calmly. Balthazar was ashamed. He had assumed that the boss had lost his touch, that he'd gotten reckless and considered his position unassailable. But he was wrong. Dead wrong. The boss knew. He knew the risks, he knew the danger, and here was Balthazar lying to his face.

"Of course, boss. I'm sure you're right. Perhaps I haven't got my ear to ground enough. I'll be sure to find out who knows."

"Yes, good. Find out soon will you? I'm going away for a while, in a few weeks."

"What? Where?"

"Oh, just some inter-department thing. An update on 'key changes to the system', or some such bullshit. You know how it is. Anyway, I'd like to know where things stand before I leave." This was bad. The boss can't leave when his position is so vulnerable. Tantalus was one thing, but he had no idea what Peri knew, or how she was involved. Maybe if he knew, he wouldn't leave. But he couldn't tell him now, then he would know he had been lying. If it all went to shit none of that would matter. If the boss is out, then so is he. Balthazar decided he had time. Time to save himself and the boss.

"I'll get right on it, boss. Leave it to me."

"Thank you Zar, that'll be all." Balthazar left. Outside the office he went straight to work, starting with Heather.

"Heather, call me a meeting with the top generals. Do it quietly, and don't invite Stratus or Dave."

"OK, why not those two?"

"Stratus works with Tantalus, and Dave… well, Dave's just a prick. I mean, what kind of demon is called fucking Dave, honestly?"

“Got it.” Heather would normally have further questions, she would normally have more quips and be more resistive, seeing as she didn’t actually work for Balthazar. There was something in the frantic, yet businesslike manner with which he gave the orders though. Heather could tell something serious was going down.

“That demon you spoke to earlier, her name is Peri, if she comes back, say nothing and call me immediately. And if you see Tantalus—”

“I know, Tantalus is a cunt.”

“Indeed.” Balthazar trailed off, his eyes darting back and forth, planning.

“So, are you cancelling the party tonight?” she asked.

“It’s not a—no, I don’t want Peter getting any ideas. Set the meeting for first thing in the morning.”

“Of course.”

“Thank you, Heather.” Balthazar said as he left, leaving Heather stunned. He had never thanked her before. He had never said anything nice to her before. Heather began making the necessary calls when she heard a dull vibration coming from the boss’ office. Seemed like he was listening to music, but he never did this at work.

Inside his office the devil was lying on his makeshift couch, taking deep breaths. He let his eyelids grow heavy, but he didn’t shut his eyes. He let his body weight sink into the couch underneath, surrendering his tension. The music played as he continued to deepen his breath, his eyes opening and shutting ever so gently, like the flowing tide, before finally kissing shut, as he entered a deep and peaceful slumber.

25

Karen was off speaking with some of her colleagues, leaving Peter standing alone at the bar, casually sipping his vodka coke, trying to make it last. It was her office Christmas party, the third that she had dragged Peter to. He didn't like them. He didn't like the people she worked with. The men reminded him of the idiots he went to school with; the sporty guys who thought the height of humour was taking the piss out of someone's shoes. The women were worse, albeit subtler. He could tell that when they would look him up and down, they were comparing him to Karen and wondering how on Earth their precious Karen could end up with someone like him.

She was different around them. She was nice, friendly, charming even. This made Peter out to be the ungrateful layabout. The one who didn't know how to get along with her friends. Karen had stopped trying to include him. The only reason she still brought him along was because she felt she had to, even though she would just leave him at the bar by himself. This was before the days you could pull out your phone and pretend to text or mindlessly scroll.

"Peter!" a voice shouted. *Ah fuck,* Peter thought, as he was approached by Kevin — or rather, Kev — and his wife, Becca.

"Hello, Kev."

"How you doing, pal? Long time, no see!" Kev said, loudly. Kev was loud.

"Yeah, it's probably been about a year," replied Peter, dryly referencing the previous office party he was dragged to. Kev burst out laughing in a manner that was disproportionate to how funny the joke was.

"This guy, huh? Hey, listen, how's the music business?" Kev asked. Peter glanced at Becca, who, like him, was also being dragged to these parties while wishing she could be anywhere else.

"I wouldn't really know Kev. I mainly play weddings in a band."

"Ah well, things'll pick up, eh?" Kev tended to finish sentences with a question, but he wasn't really asking anything. At least, he never cared to hear an answer.

"Hello Becca. How are you?" Peter said, wishing to distract from his sinking music career.

"I'm good, thanks," she said, from behind her wine glass. Peter liked Becca; she was the only one here that seemed like a real person to him. Everyone else seemed to only be pretending to be real, behaving in a way that they thought was normal. Becca was genuine.

"Ha, this guy, eh? Moving in on my wife, are you?" Kev butted in again. Then he laughed at his own joke — if you could call it that — even more than he had done before.

"Ha, yeah, watch out." Peter put little effort into joshing, but Kev didn't seem to notice his apathy.

"Oh, listen, we've got some news, don't we?"

"Do you?"

"We do. Go on sweetie, tell him." Kev nudged Becca.

"What about Karen?" said Becca clearly uncomfortable about being put on the spot.

"Ah, we'll tell her in a minute, won't we? Go on."

"OK… uh… we're having a baby."

"Fuck yeah, turns out my boys are decent swimmers after all, eh?" Again, Kev erupted into laughter.

"Congratulations," Peter said, reaching into his bank of human responses and forcing a smile. Peter hadn't cared much about having children when he was younger, all he cared about was 'making it'. Recently he had been thinking about it more, and had raised it a few times with Karen, to little avail.

"Thank you," Becca replied. Peter could see she wasn't that excited. Looking at her eyes there was almost a sense of fear, as if she was petrified at the thought of unleashing another Kev unto the world.

Karen and Peter arrived home exhausted. Karen had ignored Peter all night but that was fine with him. If they don't engage with each other then they can't fall out. Peter sat on the couch as Karen went to the kitchen to prepare a nightcap. Peter was still thinking about Becca as Karen placed a drink in front of him.

"Interesting news about Kev and Becca," he said, as Karen sat on her chair with a heavy sigh.

"Don't start Peter."

"Don't start what?"

"You know what? We've talked about it already, it's a non-starter."

"You said if we sorted some things out—"

"And we haven't Peter. We haven't sorted anything out. Actually, let me clarify that, *you* haven't sorted anything out. We're still here, still in the same situation."

"Yes, I know. I'm sorry. I wasn't trying to start anything," Peter stammered.

"Good." They sat in silence for a while after that. Peter couldn't remember what changed in his life. Perhaps it was his failing career that made him a family man. Perhaps he just wanted something fruitful in his life, something he could contribute to the world. If it couldn't be his music then maybe it could be his children. Maybe they could be better than him. Maybe he could hang his hat on his successful children and find some contentedness in that. Then again, maybe Karen was right. He looked around the shabby flat that they lived in. He thought about his bank account and how long it had been since his balance included a comma.

Peter finished his drink with a final gulp and left the room without saying anything.

26

The smell burned the nostrils, the place was dark even by hell's standards, and there was little life here amongst the dead.

"What is this place?" Peter asked, trying not to sound too trepidatious.

"Just a change of scenery," Balthazar replied hastily, as he looked at the drab surroundings. Peter looked at him.

"Were you getting tired of that bartender?"

"Yes. Yes, I was," Balthazar admitted immediately. "I mean what a prick though. I'm a fucking demon and he has the audacity to question me? I could've drunk that entire fucking bar and still went to war that night."

"Well, at least you're over it," Peter joked.

"Don't get smart, Peter." Balthazar wasn't upset though, he smirked, noticeably at Peter's dry humour. "Let's find a booth, I don't like standing at this bar. It's… unsanitary."

"I wouldn't have thought that would be a major concern down here. But what do I know?"

"Exactly, what do you know? I think you're finally starting to get it." They took their drinks and walked together to find a place to sit. Balthazar sat with his back to the wall, persistently looking left and right. He seemed wound-up a little today, but Peter couldn't tell if this was normal or not. Since walking here Peter had been mainly concerned with himself, which he felt was justified. Balthazar seemed to be scoping the place.

"Are you… looking for someone?" Peter asked. Balthazar snapped back to Peter, a little confused.

"What? No, no, just, you know… can't be too careful around these parts, you never know who's about," he explained, unconvincingly.

"Uh huh." Peter sipped at his drink, eyeing Balthazar suspiciously. He figured there was more to the story, but he didn't feel like pursuing. It likely had nothing to do with him anyway. Balthazar was a demon with many responsibilities, yet here he was taking the time to celebrate with Peter. "So, it isn't weird for you to be drinking with a human?" Peter asked, wishing to change the subject.

"Nah. It's pretty common practice. All part of keeping the workers happy. Well, sane, at least."

"I see." Peter had a follow-up question but he didn't want to ask. He knew what Balthazar's reaction would be. Something compelled him, however, he had to know.

"So, can demons… you know… sleep with humans." Balthazar nearly spat his drink out. At first Peter thought he was furious, but once Balthazar had carefully put his drink down, he erupted in laughter.

"You are unbelievable! I don't think I've ever met anyone as obsessed with getting down and dirty as you are. Incredible, simply incredible!" Balthazar laughed some more and was beginning to draw the attention of those around them.

"So, is this you making your move? Because I see you more as a friend."

"Forget about it."

"Ah come on, I'm kidding. Look, most demons are repulsed by the idea, but for the few who feel like a power trip, it's physically impossible. As much as I would like to blow your tiny little mind with the details, I doubt you could comprehend the reasons. Just remember, you're not really here. Not in flesh and blood. It's all an illusion Peter," Balthazar explained, and Peter nodded.

With all that had been going on, he had managed to briefly forget his own mortality. He felt alive, but it was just that, a feeling. Peter instinctively rubbed his hands together, feeling the flesh, and the warmth underneath. He felt alive.

"Did it work?" Peter asked abruptly. He had been avoiding the question, he feared the answer.

"Hard to say, Peter," Balthazar said. Peter let a sigh of relief escape under his breath. "Even if it did work there's no telling how well it worked, or that it'll keep working. We'll have to wait and see."

"Right. I've got a stay of execution then?" Peter feebly attempted to joke.

"It's not like that Peter, you're already dead. It's more like a stay of eternal suffering."

"You said it wasn't eternal."

"I know, I know. It just sounds better. What am I supposed to say instead? An undefined time of suffering after which there's just nothing. It's not exactly snappy is it?"

"Good point. I guess it does sound catchier, from a marketing perspective anyway."

"Now you're getting it." Balthazar chuckled. They drank for a while longer. Balthazar was extolling stories of the 'good old days' when he and the boss and were just some up-and-comers. Grafting, fighting, and winning their way to the top. Peter didn't care much for the topic of conversation, not least because he disliked hearing about other people's successes. He did, however, like to see Balthazar in this mood. Happy, enthused, and almost joyous as he detailed all his triumphs through the years. For a moment, Peter forgot that this figure would be the one to put him back into a pool of suffering for millennia to come. Peter was musing about his fate when Balthazar cut himself off mid-diatribe,

"Hold on, I gotta talk to this guy. Just hang out here. Don't move." Balthazar made off quickly and caught up with a figure near the bar, leaving Peter on his own. It was the first time he had been alone outside his room. It made him uneasy, he felt vulnerable. The figure and Balthazar were still talking — amicably, it seemed — when another figure appeared and sat next to Peter.

"I hope I'm not interrupting."

“Uh…” Peter had no words.

“Are you a friend of Balthazar’s?”

“Um… yes,” Peter said hesitantly. He looked over at Balthazar, trying to get his attention telepathically. But apparently that wasn’t a power he had down here, as Balthazar never looked around.

“Yes, I see. My name is Stratus, I’m a general of Balthazar’s.” The figure outstretched a hand to Peter, but Peter remembered what Balthazar had told him earlier.

“Are you Tantalus?” Peter asked. The figure was shocked at Peter’s ability to see through his guise. Tantalus had underestimated him.

“I… what? Who…” Tantalus began, but gave up quickly. “Fuck it, whatever. Yes, my name is Tantalus. I guess Balthazar warned you about me and you’re probably going to tell him I was here, so let me be quick.” Tantalus leaned in closer. Peter again tried to will Balthazar to look their way, but to no avail. “You can’t trust Balthazar. You can’t believe what he tells you. Your life, and death, is not as it seems. I know there’s no reason for you to believe me, but when Balthazar’s returns, ask him how you died.”

“I know how I died.”

“Do you really?” Tantalus said mysteriously.

“Yes. Yes, I do,” Peter replied, matter-of-factly, much to Tantalus’ disappointment.

“Fuck’s sake. Just ask him the fucking question, you idiot.” And with that, Tantalus ran off. Peter was left alone again, thinking about the day he died. Sitting at his Baby Grand piano looking at the coffee rings, alone in his grey, dreary flat with just a stray cat for company. Peter's last memory was of feeling completely uninspired, before slipping into darkness. Balthazar returned, awakening Peter from his daydream.

"Sorry about that."

"No problem. Hey, how did I die?"

Balthazar looked at Peter utterly amazed. "I can't honestly remember Peter. It was either a heart-attack or a brain aneurysm. One of those, quick, sudden things you know."

"I see."

"Why are you asking all of a sudden? You remember it don't you? You must remember collapsing at least."

"Sure." Peter was willing to let it go. He was debating whether or not to tell Balthazar about Tantalus when Balthazar figured it out.

"Did someone speak to you?"

"Uh..." Peter was stumbling for an answer, but he had already taken too long.

"I knew it. Was it Tantalus? Peri?"

"Who the fuck is Peri?"

"Tantalus then. What did I tell you about him?"

"He's a cunt."

"Correct. Don't listen to a word he says. He's after the boss' job. He'll do anything to get it." Balthazar waved it off as if that were the end of it.

"What does that have to do with me?"

"Let me be clear, Peter." Balthazar was no longer the friend telling stories, he had resorted back to the demon caretaker. “I don’t have to explain fucking *anything* to you. You want me to go through centuries of hellish politics? Or do you want to just trust me?”

“I want to just trust you.” Peter knew it was pointless to try and take it any further.

“Good answer. Now c’mon, finish your drink already so we can get another. We’re fucking celebrating remember.”

Peter did as he was told, and dutifully emptied his glass. Balthazar got another round by summoning the bartender, rather than going to the bar. It was evident he didn’t want to leave Peter alone again, for even a moment. Peter’s mind was still racing. He was still questioning everything Balthazar had ever told him, trying to poke holes, trying to find the missing details to fill in the gaps. But none of it made sense. He was a dead soul writing music for the devil. None of it made any fucking sense.

Peter submitted to the alcohol and they both got good and drunk. Balthazar told more stories, and Peter complained about his life on Earth, mainly about Karen. The more he told, the more Balthazar could see how horrible she was, and by extension, how horrible his life had been. None of it surprised him. *Perhaps he already knew,* thought Peter. In any case, their understanding of one another grew as the night wore on, and by the time Balthazar dropped Peter off at his room, he felt like he could trust him again. More than anyone else down here anyway.

Balthazar strode off home as Peter walked into his room. There, he could see a box on his piano, elaborately decorated with a bow around it. Peter walked over, cautiously, looking around the room to make sure no one else was there. He opened the box, half-expecting it to explode in his face. It didn't. Peter looked down and inside the box there was a fleshlight. Peter read the tag attached it, which read, 'Go nuts you filthy little pervert! From, Zar'.

27

Balthazar surveyed the room with an accusing eye. Around half the demons there were simply confused or oblivious, but the other half looked visibly nervous. There were about a dozen of them seated in the room, and Balthazar stood over them, piercing them with his gaze. Balthazar knew that some here would have met with Tantalus, and he was prepared for that. Scanning his eyes to the back of the room Balthazar noticed that Dave was present. Heather would never have gone against his commands — Balthazar hated to admit it, but she was extremely good at her job — so he must have heard about the meeting from another general and tagged along.

"What's the meaning of this Balthazar?" It was one of the nervous generals. Perhaps he feels that going on the offensive would prove his innocence. It didn't work.

"Excellent question but make it your last," Balthazar sneered. He was angry and out for blood. "As some of you will be aware," he paused for a long time to look directly at all those he suspected. "There is a plot to put us out of power." There were a few gasps and some muttering, along with some guilty eyes staring at the ground.

Balthazar continued, "Frankly, I don't give a fuck if you're in on it or not. I don't care about any of you enough to take it personally. But let me be clear, there is only one winning side in all of this and you're currently on it. Things will go a lot smoother if you stay on it, but I can't stop you from choosing incorrectly. I've brought you all here to say just that. Stay with us if you want to keep your job. Otherwise, I'll fucking destroy you all." Balthazar did not raise his voice, nor did he bang the table or show any signs of aggression. He was calm, cold, and calculating. Moreover, he was thoroughly enjoying himself.

"What kind of plot?" asked Dave, from the back.

"Just shut the fuck up Dave. From now until the end of existence, shut the fuck up!" Balthazar had allowed Dave to shake him from his cool demeanour and that upset him more than hearing Dave's voice. It was a perfectly valid question; he just really didn't like Dave. Balthazar calmed himself, before looking at the whole room.

"I don't want confessions, or apologies or pledges of fealty. Just fucking behave yourselves, and we'll have no issues." Balthazar looked at every demon in turn, searching for signs of dissent or rebellion. He could see none and was satisfied that the message had gotten across.

"You may all leave and go back to work." They all began to stand and leave. "Oh, and no one tell Stratus about anything that happened here. Dave, I'm looking at you here. Nothing personal, I just don't trust you." Dave opened his mouth to talk but was cut-off by Balthazar's stare before he could even start. He simply nodded, then left with everyone else.

Balthazar took a seat in the now empty room, considering his next move. More than likely, he wouldn't have to speak to Stratus at all. Tantalus wouldn't be much of a problem without the support he needed. Peri could still be a problem, however. She didn't need Tantalus, or the support of any generals. Tantalus was a coward, and could do nothing without a small army behind him — or rather, in front of him — but Peri had the balls needed to pull this off by herself. Leaning forward in his chair, Balthazar considered his options, and realised there weren't many.

First things first, he thought to himself, he would have to deal with Tantalus. He was almost licking his lips at the prospect of tearing down the little cunt.

28

As Peter lay on his bed feeling thoroughly satisfied with himself — the fleshlight, lying, abused, on the floor — he couldn't help but think back to the time that Karen walked in on him masturbating. He was initially home alone, unemployed as usual, and Karen wasn't due back from work for another hour. This meant he had some time to play with.

Peter fetched his laptop, brought up a private browsing window and got to work finding just the right video. In the end — after searching through several pages — he had several videos to work with, spread across several tabs. First, he had selected a couple of videos from his favourite categories. Then, he spent some time window shopping through the recently added pages. Already a little hard and excited from the search, Peter was ready to go as he removed all of his clothes. It was unnecessary to be completely naked, but when he had time, Peter much preferred this to banging out a quick one with his trousers round his ankles while trying to avoid getting cum on his shirt.

After he had finished, Peter was reaching for the tissues, tactically placed on his left-hand side, when he heard the bedroom door slam shut. Peter jumped up, turned around and saw Karen glaring at him. She had her arms folded, and was gently tapping her foot, looking like a stereotypical mum in an old American sitcom. Peter was speechless, he just stood there, his erection slowly fading while dripping cum onto the carpet.

Later, they were both sitting in the living room, waiting for the takeout to arrive. Peter was supposed to cook tonight but Karen had told him not to, even after he had showered and subsequently washed his hands another several times. The silence was killing Peter, he had expected Karen to chew him out, to scream at him like she normally did. Instead, she sat with a far-away look as her tea went cold in her hands. Every now and then Peter looked over for signs of life, but he would quickly look away, not wishing to make eye contact. Eventually, she spoke.

"You seemed to… enjoy that. Like, really enjoy that," she said, maintaining her far-away look. Peter was bemused.

"Excuse me?" Peter looked at Karen, but she did not return his gaze.

"You were just… you were just really into it," she explained further.

"I'm not sure what you're getting at." Peter was growing concerned. Karen met his gaze, not with anger, but with something that looked akin to hurt.

"Do you like masturbating more than sex?" she asked, point-blank. Peter was stunned. This was not a question he was expecting, nor was it one he had ever considered. Of course he didn't, he knew that he didn't. It was a ridiculously easy question to answer and yet, he couldn't get the words out.

"Well?" Karen prompted, shaking Peter out of his stupor.

"No, obviously not. How can you ask that?"

"You don't make those noises in bed. You're never that excited when we're together."

"We haven't even been together in months." Peter cursed himself as soon as the words left his mouth. As the words returned to him, they sounded worse than when he thought of them.

"Oh, so it's my fault?"

"No, that's not what I meant. It's just… I didn't even think you enjoyed having sex with me."

"It's not that I don't enjoy it Peter. I thought you did though."

"Jesus Christ. I can't believe we're having this conversation." Peter stood up and began pacing. Karen watched him, sipping her tea. "Are you telling me you don't enjoy masturbating? That you don't cry out when you orgasm?" Peter challenged.

"Of course I do Peter, but it's different."

"How so?" Peter had stopped pacing. His defensiveness had turned to anger.

“I don’t orgasm when we have sex. You do. And when you do, you don’t make the kind of noises I just heard from you upstairs. It seems to me you’d rather finish in your own hand than inside me. How can I not take that personally?” Karen still wasn’t shouting, she was calm, confident she was in the right. By comparison, Peter was frantic, totally unsure of himself. It was a common dynamic between the two of them.

“I don’t really know what to tell you Karen. It’s different when you’re by yourself.”

“How so?” Karen asked. Peter walked back to his chair and sat down, leaning on the edge, desperate to explain himself.

“It’s… free. I’m free of your judgement, I can let go. I’d much rather be with you, but sometimes, it’s nice to be with yourself. That’s the only way I can put it.” Peter looked pleadingly at Karen, she sipped her tea and considered his answer.

“OK. Next time we’re together, let loose. No judgement.”

“Uh… it doesn’t really work like that.”

“Let’s try anyway.” Karen had dropped her anger, looking at Peter like he was a man. Something she rarely did.

“You mean, like, right now?” Peter got a little excited at the prospect and felt the movement in his trousers. Before Karen could answer, the doorbell rang. They both looked around towards the hallway, then back to each other.

"We should probably eat first, don't you think? Maybe later," Karen said.

"Yeah, yeah. Sure." Peter took some money out Karen's purse to pay for the takeout. He returned with the food and they ate together in silence. After having a moment to think about it, Peter began dreading having sex. Karen had said no judgement but the whole point was judgement. She would be judging him the entire time, comparing his sounds, face, and body language to what she had just witnessed. Their sex life wasn't great as things were and this may just be the end of it. As he struggled with his chopsticks, Peter couldn't help but feel this wasn't his fault. He had cracked one out while home alone and now he would be on trial every time they had sex for the rest of his life.

The whole event ran through Peter's head as he sat in hell, staring at the walls. They weren't together much longer after that, for many reasons outside of their sex life. They did however have sex a few times before they split. Peter couldn't enjoy any of it, he was tense the whole time. Karen had been his only partner through his whole life. As he lay there, the heat and smell of his afterlife making him sweat and cringe, he considered that perhaps, he never had satisfying sex in his entire life.

Peter looked again at the fleshlight on the ground. *Best partner I ever had,* he thought to himself, before dismissing any thought of Karen, and falling into a peaceful sleep.

29

Balthazar was continuing his efforts to quell the uprising that was taking place against the boss, and by extension, himself. He had taken it upon himself to confront Tantalus. Not wishing to do this at work, he was currently skulking in a dive bar. This place was very foreign to Balthazar. He had been to a few dive bars in his time, but demons of his rank were rarely, if ever, seen in places as low as this. The air was stale, and the fire burned low, leaving its dejected inhabitants squinting in the shadows. The place was full of rejects. It was a home for the sick, abused, and downtrodden. It's where fallen angels land when they get their aim wrong.

Balthazar was trying to keep a low profile, but his presence was easily noticeable. Some were looking his way, but few cared enough to do anything about it. Apart from the odd murmur his presence was being ignored. *That'll do I guess,* he thought to himself as he prepared for his encounter.

Tantalus would arrive shortly, expecting to meet one of his insiders for his weekly dose of gossip from the inner workings of those in charge. Balthazar knew this meeting would be soon as he had his own insiders, and was informed of it not long after his meeting with the general. It was a harmless exercise as far as Balthazar was concerned. No one that would speak to Tantalus knew anything of consequence. Balthazar was more than happy for this insider to keep feeding him useless information. He was not here to interrupt the meeting; he was here to confront Tantalus.

He could have done so anywhere, but he had a distinct advantage in a place like this. Tantalus would be comfortable here, bolder, more willing to speak out and let something slip. In Balthazar's usual haunts, Tantalus would be coy, wary of those around him. Balthazar needed him to talk. He felt he knew his secret, but he knew it was still only a rumour. Tantalus would have to confirm it, to his face, for it to be of any use to Balthazar.

Taking a spot in the corner, with the entire place in view, Balthazar kept his head down and kept his eyes peeled. It wasn't long before he spotted a hunched figure creep into the bar. Balthazar could spot the little cunt from a mile off. Tantalus took a long look over each shoulder before settling into a booth on the opposite end of the bar. He seemed to take in the entire place and yet he never saw Balthazar. *He must be losing his touch,* Balthazar thought, before making his way over to Tantalus.

Tantalus saw him coming but he had no room to run away. He had chosen his spot carelessly so that Balthazar was between him and the exit. It would be foolish to run in any case. He didn't yet know why he was here. The best bet was to play it cool.

"Hello, Tantalus," Balthazar said, as he took a seat across from him.

"Balthazar! How lovely to see you," Tantalus exclaimed, much to Balthazar's annoyance.

"Cut the shit Tantalus. This is a shakedown, I'm here to shake you down. We're not doing a fucking tête-à-tête, OK? We're not going to have a witty fucking back and forth over cocktails, all right? So just shut the fuck up." Tantalus recoiled at Balthazar's harsh words. Tantalus knew he didn't like him; few people did. However, the utter disdain did take him by surprise a little.

"I see. Well then, what is it you want?" Tantalus steadied himself, scanning through a thousand lies in his head searching for the right one. Balthazar leaned in.

"I don't give a fuck what you're doing here. I don't care who you're meeting or what he's goin[illegible] tell you. I know you're plotting something, and I k[illegible]ose're doing it because you think that you know som[illegible]eth[illegible] Balthazar instinctively looked over his shoulder. [illegible]yone in the place was paying them little attention, so he continued, "I want to tell you, that you don't know shit. You don't have any fucking clue."

"That's all fine and dandy Balthazar—" Tantalus began but was cut-off.

"I'm not fucking finished, you little cunt. I also want to tell you, that I know *your* secret. I know what you've done to that little fucking device you cherish so much. I wanted to tell you this, not because I'm going to snitch on you or anything, but because I want you to stop. Whatever the fuck you're planning, stop." Balthazar leaned back a touch in his seat, trying to take in Tantalus and judge how his words had hit him.

Tantalus froze at this accusation. Balthazar was clearly referring to Tantalus' tool for listening to souls on Earth. His use of the device was well known but Tantalus firmly believed his tampering with it couldn't possibly be known to anyone but himself. Of course, there were rumours, but nothing substantial. In any case, this wasn't the trump card Balthazar believed it to be. Tantalus calmed himself.

"Even if those rumours were true—" Tantalus began.

"They are," Balthazar interrupted, again.

"OK, fine, they are! They are true, it's all true," conceded Tantalus, matter-of-factly. Balthazar was shocked, and it was briefly written on his face, but he quickly comp[illegible]d himself. He thought he would have to work a bit ha[illegible]o get Tantalus to admit it. This was all too easy.

"So, then you know what this could do to your reputation and—" Balthazar began.

"So fucking what?" Tantalus interrupted this time. Balthazar's shock was there for all to see and this time he didn't regain control of himself. Tantalus got the reaction he was looking for, taking the upper hand.

"I don't… what?" Balthazar stammered.

"Everyone knows Balthazar. Everyone fucking knows. Stratus knows. Your fucking boss probably knows. And you know what? None of them care. As long as the souls keep flowing nobody cares how they get here. We all keep it hush-hush for the sake of deniability. Those idiots up there have their suspicions but as long we deny it they don't care enough to challenge us. So, I'll repeat: So. Fucking. What?" By 'up there', Tantalus wasn't referring to Earth, he was referring to *up, up there*. Even Balthazar wouldn't dare spill the beans to them. That could mean the end of everything down here. Balthazar had lost his main bargaining chip, and it showed. He shrunk in his seat, and when he spoke, there was far less command in his voice.

"No matter, without the support of any generals you won't get anywhere." Balthazar had hoped to land a blow with this, but Tantalus was unfazed, he didn't even blink.

"Yes, I'm aware of your little performance the other day. Balthazar, the great leader, towering over his generals, convincing them to kowtow to his every word using nothing but his sheer charisma!"

Tantalus laughed, loudly, drawing the attention of some of those around him, "I would have preferred to have them on my side, but I don't need them. I have other allies, and their support is plenty." Balthazar sat defeated, his head hung low, and he dare not look up at Tantalus, who continued, "You know Balthazar, this may just be the greatest day of my existence. So far, that is." Tantalus stood and walked away. Balthazar was powerless, he had nothing left to say.

Tantalus knew he was missing his meeting but that didn't matter. With Balthazar's feeble attempt to shake him, he had achieved more here than he could have in a thousand meetings with his informants.

Balthazar remained in his seat for a long time. He had never felt so low, so useless. For the first time in eons, he felt like this may be the end, or at least the beginning of the end. All he had done in his entire existence was rise. Rise above those around him, those who doubted him, those who judged him and belittled him. He proved them all wrong on his way to the top, and he had remained there longer than any of them could have imagined. But nothing lasts forever. Once you reach the top the only way to go is back down. And now he could see it. The tide was coming in and it would take Balthazar with it, out to the great sea of mediocrity and anonymity. *Perhaps I should get used to places like this,* Balthazar thought, as he closed his eyes and sighed heavily.

30

Heather waited patiently at her desk for the boss to arrive. She was always at work before him. Not because she had anything to do; part of her punishment was waiting. The tedious, gnawing, waiting. Knowing that she could be anywhere else, and it wouldn't make the slightest bit of difference.

At least today she thought the boss would be in a good mood. He certainly left in one, refreshed after a long afternoon nap. *Maybe today would be slightly better than the usual,* Heather thought, realising that that was the pinnacle of what she could dream.

This part of the morning was perhaps the worst. The work was tedious but at least it was work, it kept her thoughts at bay. Heather had existed longer than most humans in history. She wasn't like these creatures that surrounded her, existing for millennia without it getting to them. Heather was mortal, and as such, there was only so much goddamn thinking she could do. She had been conscious for around four lifetimes now and her one and only hope was for it all to stop.

The boss finally arrived, but he was not in the good mood Heather had anticipated. Without looking at her, or stopping his gait, he strolled into his office ordering her to follow him in. Heather did immediately as she was told, dreading bad news but at the same time glad that the day was officially starting. Once inside, the boss stopped his hurrying and sat behind his desk. Heather stood waiting, but he was staring at the walls, deep in thought.

"Heather," he began after a while, with a long pause before continuing. "You're smart right? Like, for a human anyways." The boss always had to clarify this point when speaking to Heather, a constant reminder that she was less than him.

"I was of above average intelligence on earth." Heather had learned not to fuck around when the boss was agitated, as he currently seemed to be. Answering as accurately and matter-of-factly as possible was always the best way forward.

"I've heard that someone can get used to an alarm. So much so that they stop recognising it. Is that true?" Heather had no idea what he was getting at, but she wisely decided not to question his question.

"I can't speak for everyone but that was certainly the case with me. I often had to change my alarm," she answered. The boss seemed intrigued by her answer.

"Interesting. How often?"

"Uh… I'm not sure. Maybe every month or so. Or a little longer."

"Hmm. Yes. You are mortal though." The boss mused.

"Yes boss, so I'm told." Heather couldn't help it. She had become so used to the role she had to play it was difficult to keep it turned off. Fortunately, the boss didn't notice her sarcasm. He was still preoccupied with his own thought.

"We may have to keep the human around for a little while yet," the boss eventually said, after further consideration.

"Is that wise, sir?" Heather questioned.

"Why wouldn't it be?" the devil responded.

"Well, with all the risk surrounding him being here. Have you spoken to Balthazar about this?" Heather didn't mean to question his judgement.

"Balthazar is busy, ensuring that the risk you speak of is minimised," the devil growled.

"Of course, sir. I didn't mean to—" Heather began.

"Don't worry about it, Heather. I have much bigger issues than your insolence."

"Yes, sir." Heather was insulted and relieved at the same time. Not an unfamiliar feeling, down here. Or up there for that matter. The boss went back to his musings, as Heather stood awkwardly in the middle of the office.

"You can go Heather. I'm not expecting Balthazar today but if he does turn up then let me know immediately." The devil directed.

"Of course, Sir." Heather left quickly, eager to leave his presence and return to the nominal safety of her desk.

The rest of Heather's morning was quiet. A few calls, a bit of paperwork, nothing out of the ordinary. With the workload being so light, Heather couldn't keep herself busy enough to shut out the thoughts of the day. Once again, she found herself pouring over her life, moment after moment, analysing each decision. She had done this so often now that she could write her entire biography without any notes. Perhaps if she had been nicer to her dad, she wouldn't be down here. Perhaps if she hadn't told her ex to go fuck himself, she wouldn't be down here. Perhaps if she went to church more often — or actually believed in any of it — she wouldn't be down here. It was all pointless conjecture. Heather had been here long enough, and met enough other souls, to know that there was no reason. There was no grand scheme of checks and balances, no scorekeeping, no ranking, no nothing. You lived, you died, and in all likelihood, you ended up here.

Heather had died young. Well, *young-ish*, at thirty-seven. Her death was an accident. A random, avoidable occurrence without purpose or meaning. On Earth she became another statistic for traffic casualties. Her lasting legacy being a number on a spreadsheet. In the context of the universe, she became another tiny variable in the vast, unending equation of chaos that drove the whole tragedy of life forward. Forever forward, towards nothing in particular. *What a fucking waste,* Heather thought to herself, before getting another call. Her one and only hope was for it all to stop.

31

Peri strode into the meeting room with her usual confidence. She took a seat without waiting to be asked and stared Balthazar down with an amusing smile. Balthazar had asked her here before his encounter with Tantalus. He couldn't call it off, but he had wanted to. It was stupid of him to assume he would have dealt with Tantalus so easily. Now that he was here, he didn't know what his plan was. Peri knew all this, of course. And she was enjoying every fucking second.

"Hello, Peri," he opened meekly.

"Hello, Balthazar," she replied, happy that he had spoken first.

"I guess you've heard that I met with Tantalus."

"Yes. He told me everything. I think he's in love with me," Peri said, matter-of-factly. Balthazar laughed. He didn't mean to, but he couldn't help reacting instinctively.

"I'm sorry I—"

"Don't worry about it. I laughed myself, just not to his face."

"Sure, sure. I'm a little surprised you agreed to meet. I'm even more surprised you came given everything."

Balthazar knew he had no play. He was going through the motions, letting Peri get her kicks.

"You assume we have nothing to talk about it?" she asked.

"Well, no not really. As much as it fucking pains to me say it, the little cunt got the better of me. There's no reason to talk to me except to gloat."

"Maybe that's what I'm doing," said Peri, her smile growing.

"So that's it then. You're going to follow that squirmy fuck all the way to the top. And then what? You're going to play second fiddle?" Balthazar challenged.

"It works for you," she joked.

"I'm not second fiddle to a cunt. Totally different prospect."

"You're absolutely right," Peri said, leaning back in her chair. Balthazar didn't understand this concession. Peri's smirk took on a different meaning as he surveyed the figure opposite him.

"What's going on? Are you making a play right now?" Balthazar asked, hoping to shake Peri in some way. But she wasn't ruffled.

"Well, right now I was enjoying the foreplay, but I had heard rumours you were keen to skip that," she teased.

"I understand you're joking, but my sexual proclivity is unquestioned, and I will not tolerate any slander," Balthazar replied sternly. Peri held her hands up in apology. Balthazar continued, "Perhaps you could walk me through it, because I'm a little confused." Balthazar let go of any pretence that he was in control. This was Peri's meeting now. He was just along for the ride. Peri leaned forward to assume that control.

"Why did you want to me meet here? In your offices, rather than some dive joint like Tantalus?" Balthazar considered this for a moment. He hadn't given it much thought at the time.

"Well, Tantalus is a—"

"Cunt. Yes, literally the entire Underworld is aware of this fact. But that's not the difference. You don't take Tantalus seriously, and you shouldn't. He's just a pest, someone you want to get rid of. He's not worthy of your time in a place of business," Peri explained on Balthazar's behalf.

"And you are?" Balthazar teased.

"You can't go back to foreplay Balthazar, we're in it now. The answer is yes. Yes, I am." Peri leaned back again, satisfied with her comments, knowing she had Balthazar on a hook.

"All right." Balthazar threw his hands in the air. "Shoot your shot."

"You didn't get the better of Tantalus because you thought you knew his secret. Unfortunately, it was the one everyone else already knew. He likes it that way because it hides his real secret," Peri explained and Balthazar's eyes widened.

"His real secret?" he whispered, with bated breath.

"Yes. Getting into the ear of humans and leading them to temptation is a nice little gimmick. But that's not how he gets such great volume through the door," Peri began to explain as Balthazar's jaw dropped. He thought he must have looked idiotic, but he didn't care. This could be his saving grace. He could be back in the game. He didn't dare speak, waiting like a dog for the scraps of intel being fed to him. Peri continued, "I'm not going to tell you what he really does. Not right now anyway, not until I get some assurances. You're a smart boy and maybe you've figured it out already but I'm not giving you confirmation yet."

"What do you want?" Balthazar blurted out immediately. Ordinarily he would sit back, consider, and move cautiously in any arrangement. But these were extenuating circumstances. Now was not the time for caution or consideration. Now was the time to move.

"It should be obvious Balthazar. I want a fucking job," answered Peri. Balthazar looked at Peri and admired her. She had played this to perfection. Balthazar would have given her his job at this point. Balthazar admired her cunning. He admired the confident way she waltzed around, with complete faith in her own abilities. Most of all, he admired the fact she was willing to throw Tantalus into a pit of fire if it meant she would finally be recognised. Balthazar could see why Tantalus had fallen for her. His own feelings are not so easily swayed, but still, he admired her.

32

The night that Karen and Peter split was the worst of Peter's life. And that was really saying something. It had been awful for many reasons. It started first thing in the morning and continued all through the day. To start with, as Karen was leaving for work in the morning, she brushed against the curtains, leaving a small gap which let the sun come through straight into Peter's eyes. Having been gigging late the night before, Peter was due for a lie in. And now he wasn't getting it.

Waking far too early, Peter went to the kitchen to find that the cereal was finished and there was no milk for his coffee. Peter opted for some toast instead, but the butter was almost finished so he had to desperately scrape the tub and even then, he barely managed to cover the bread.

The toothpaste was also almost finished. Peter had to roll it up just to get a minimal amount onto his toothbrush. Peter sat in his living room, trying to remember a worse morning, and coming up short. He had hoped to be fresh for the afternoon when he had a meeting at the bank. With the gig work not panning out, Peter had decided to establish an entertainment business and he needed some capital to get it off the ground. Initially, Peter considered asking Karen's parents, but they had already given them so much, which went towards the house. So, he was trying to get a loan.

Peter arrived at the bank, in his drab suit, tired, hungry, and desperate. In the end, it mattered not how he presented himself, the decision had already been made and it didn't go Peter's way. He was too exhausted to be upset. Forgoing a taxi, he drudged home in the rain.

For a while, Peter thought he started to feel depressed. But after some consideration, he realised it would be insulting to those actually struggling with depression to call it that. He was just sad. Extremely, enormously sad. It was boring. It was an uninteresting conclusion. At least depression would give him some kind of character edge, some kind of struggling artist vibe. But it wasn't true. He was just sad.

Karen was due home late that day, and was going to eat at work, so Peter made himself dinner. It was a paltry meal of premade chicken drumsticks which he picked up at the corner shop. Peter ate them cold, straight out the packet, while tuning the radio between stations so he could listen to the static, in a vain attempt to keep out any intrusive, negative thoughts.

The front door opened and gently clicked shut as Karen apprehensively meandered into the living room. There was no way she could have known what happened today at the bank, but she had a strong feeling. History had told her it would not go well, and her suspicions were proven correct as she saw Peter, sitting with a cold, blank stare, listening to the static on the radio. Peter did not look up at her. He was sadder for her than he was for himself. Karen was no angel, but she wasn't an inherently bad person… at least, Peter didn't think she was. She had hitched her wagon to Peter's life, she had entwined their fates and rested all hope in him. Now he had to disappoint her, again.

Karen walked over and turned the radio off. Still, Peter did not stir. Karen took a seat on the chair next to Peter.

"So, how did it go at the bank?" Karen began, with no hope in her voice. Peter did not respond. He just sat and stared. "I see." Karen carefully smoothed her skirt and clasped her hands, like she was a schoolteacher who was not angry, but just disappointed. "Peter, I think this is the last time. I think from now on, your failures will be your own. I'm leaving you Peter." Karen had more to say but she was waiting for Peter's reaction to this news. It never came. Peter was still as a mountain. "Fine, if you have nothing to say to me, I'll just keep going. I had hoped this could work out Peter, I really did. I've known for a few years now that there was nothing here for me, but I stayed. I stayed because part of me believed you could turn your life around. Maybe part of it was pity, also… I don't know." Karen was calm. She had practised this many times and the occasion wasn't too big for her. "I'm going to stay with a friend tonight and tomorrow night. The day after, I'll be back here at noon, and I expect you to be gone. I expect all of your stuff, what little there is, to be gone. Listen to me very carefully Peter. When I return, I want there to be no trace of you. I want to walk into this house and have it be like you never existed. I gave you some of my best years and I'll never get them back. But I want to move on immediately, I want to forget about you instantly. Do you understand?" Karen finished.

Peter's eyes drifted across towards Karen, but they stayed down, never meeting hers. He gave the slightest hint of a nod. He hadn't zoned out completely, he had heard everything Karen had said. Peter felt nothing as she talked. He spent the time wondering if he had become numb, or if he had already stopped loving Karen. Could it really be the latter? Could he have moved so quickly from not loving her to feeling nothing for her? Surely there would be some residual feelings, a modicum of affection, a crumb of empathy left over from the shitshow that was their relationship. And yet here he sat, unfeeling and uncaring.

Karen packed some of her things into a small suitcase and left without saying another word. Peter had been sat in his chair for a long time now and he had gone stiff. With great effort, and with his bones creaking, he lifted himself to his feet. Standing in the middle of the room, wallowing in the empty silence, he removed all of his clothes. He went into the bathroom completely naked and started to run a bath. He wasn't really sure what he was doing but he was sure in his actions, he was resolute. He took the spare razors from the drawer and carefully removed a single blade.

Peter shut his eyes as he listened to the rushing water from the tap. It was oddly tranquil. He was transported from the murkiness of his current surroundings to a tropical location from a shampoo advert. It gave him a brief bit of light, but the darkness was too overwhelming. Peter opened his eyes and stared at the bath. Surely this was too dramatic. It wouldn't be in keeping with his character. People would be confused rather than upset if they found him, 'Godfather' style, in the bath with his wrists cut. Peter turned his eyes to the bathroom mirror. The more appropriate way to do it was here, naked, and vulnerable, standing on the cold tiles of the bathroom floor.

Peter carefully placed the razor between his thumb and forefinger. Then he gently hovered the razor above his arm, tracing the lines of the veins in a dry run. With the bath still running, Peter breathed deeply and steadied himself. Then he spaced out.

It was only for a fraction of a second. But when he came to, standing there with the razor still in his hand, he was a different person.

Gone was the nihilistic world view that nothing mattered, replaced by a 'fuck you' attitude that burned deep inside him. Fuck them all. Fuck the producers who never believed in his talent, fuck his parents for forcing him to learn piano in the first place, fuck his teacher and her fucking cane, fuck Karen because… well, just fuck Karen.

They all wanted this for him. They all believed this would be his predictable end. Well, fuck them. His very existence would serve as his defiance. He would go on living for the sole purpose of pissing off everyone who never thought he would make it this far.

Peter placed the razor down on the sink and walked over to the bath. He tested the water with his hand, turned the tap off, and then eased himself in. Breathing in the steam and surrendering his body to the water.

33

Balthazar had met the boss in high spirits. The threat had been neutralised and all they had to do was give a high-ranking position to an extremely competent demon — Peri had some other minor requests, but they were more than reasonable. The boss was pleased, he was just about to leave for the next few weeks, and this was welcome news. He had been distracted though, and when Balthazar found out why, his spirits faded.

Apparently, the music written by Peter had lost its effectiveness almost immediately. Which meant that if the boss wanted to continue using it, he would have to keep Peter around indefinitely. This was unthinkable, given the risk associated with having him around. He had to go. And Balthazar was the one who had to do it.

Peter was sitting at the piano, playing around with the keys, as Balthazar sat on the bed. Currently, Peter was unaware of his impending fate, but that wasn't the worst part. Balthazar had made up his mind to tell Peter the truth. It was set to be one of the hardest things he ever had to do.

"So, what's happening? Did the boss like the music?" Peter asked, blissful in his ignorance.

"Yes, he did Peter. He fucking loved it, actually. But—" Peter stopped playing with the keys and turned to look at Balthazar. He wasn't expecting a 'but'.

"But?" Peter inquired.

"It worked, initially, remarkably. But it wore off, and it did so quickly," Balthazar responded, Peter raised his eyebrows with mild shock.

"I thought that would happen but not quite so quickly."

"Well, apparently being an immortal and powerful being means that your ears are more finely tuned than your average human," Balthazar explained, as Peter nodded.

"I see. So, what does this mean? Do I need to write more? Does he need to see me?" Peter was getting excited at the prospect, but Balthazar raised a hand to stop him.

"Peter, you have to go back." It was blunt, and Peter was surprised at how hard it hit him. He'd long given up on the idea of bargaining in this place. This was the only possible outcome for him, and he had come to terms with it. Still, the suddenness of it was hard to take.

"Right. Got it." Peter rubbed his forehead and tried to rationalise his eminent demise. At least when he died, he never saw it coming. He never had to deal with knowing it was over. Even worse, this time he knew what awaited him. He began to question things again. "So, why do I have to go back? I mean, the boss still needs me, right?" Peter pleaded.

"There's too much risk, Peter."

"Is this about that Tantalus guy?"

"No, I've dealt with that. But there will be others. We won't always be so lucky."

"Oh, this is lucky is it?" Peter scoffed.

"Peter—" Balthazar began, but Peter cut him off.

"It's fine Balthazar, I get it. You don't owe me anything. None of this is your fault, I'm just... disappointed." Peter stared at the floor, as he made some realisations. "I know that this isn't any sort of life, but I was getting used to it, you know?" Peter said, helplessly.

"I'm sorry Peter." Balthazar was sincere, but Peter wasn't really paying attention to him, preoccupied as he was with his own mortality.

"Don't worry, you don't have anything to be sorry for, right? It's just a job or some such shit," Peter quipped.

"Or some such shit, yeah," Balthazar agreed, and then steadied himself. "Peter, there's more."

Now Peter looked up, and he was taken aback by the figure sitting across from him. Gone was the striking, confident, jokester that he had first met in that imaginary café all that time ago. He was replaced by a sulking, apologetic figure. Shrunken, by some form of guilt that Peter could not see.

"What is it?"

"I haven't told you everything. I haven't been honest with you." Peter was concerned now. *What was he talking about? Was his fate worse than what he thought?* Peter remained silent as Balthazar continued, "How old do you think you are, Peter? Or rather, how old were you when you died?"

"I was forty-three. Why do you ask? What the fuck is going on?" Peter asked, exasperated.

"Peter… you died when you were twenty-eight." Balthazar let the announcement sit in the air between them. It was slowly absorbed by Peter, who understood what he was saying but it didn't make any sense.

"What the fuck are you talking about?"

"The night Karen left you. You went through with it. There was no change of heart. No epiphany. You died that night, in that bathroom," Balthazar explained. Peter stood up and started pacing the room.

"I… but I didn't. I kept going, I had a life. It wasn't a very good one, but it happened!" Peter exclaimed.

"No Peter, it didn't. Everything after that night. It was made up… by me. I invented that life for you. Then I gave you the memories," Balthazar clarified. Peter hunched to the floor in a low squat, his head in his hands, trying to make sense of it all.

"So, you're telling me, that the last fifteen years of my life — which were fucking miserable by the way — didn't actually happen? I was a fucking mess! My life was fucked! I was lonely, depressed. Those were the worst years of my life." Peter was growing in rage as his understanding grew.

"Your life wasn't exactly great before then either," Balthazar tried to explain.

"Really? Fuck you. I mean, really? That's your get-out-of-jail card? That's what clears your conscience? My life was already shit so what's another fifteen years of misery. Fuck me. You couldn't have given me *some* happy memories? Just the occasional bit of good news, no?" Peter was pacing again, his mind whirring like a carousel. Balthazar said nothing, he had no defence. Peter slowed down and took deep breathes to prevent himself from hyperventilating. If that was even possible here.

"Why? Balthazar, why?" Peter pleaded.

"You weren't any use to me the way you were, a suicidal failed musician, bordering on nihilism. You would have gone straight back to the pool of souls. You would have accepted that fate immediately. I needed someone with a little fight in them, someone who wanted to exist," Balthazar explained further.

"Fucking hell. And that's what you came up with? My whole revelation that night, that was the best you could do?" Peter asked. Balthazar shrugged.

"I didn't have a lot of time… I—" Balthazar tried to defend himself.

"Oh, fuck off." Peter walked back over to the piano and sat down.

"I'm sorry, Peter. Really, I am." Balthazar's apology was genuine, but he wasn't asking for forgiveness. He wasn't trying to appease his own conscience either, he said it because what the fuck else was he supposed to say.

"I spaced out that night. Right as I was about to do it. Was that you? Like, what was that, just bad editing?" Peter asked.

"Kind of yeah, it's hard to stitch a fake memory to a real one."

"Fuck me. Why didn't you pull Martin Scorsese out the pool, maybe he could have helped you out?" Peter laughed a little at his own joke, as did Balthazar.

"He's actually still alive, so… yeah." They both laughed again.

"So, I really did it. I always wondered why I changed my mind. It wasn't regret, really, more… curiosity. Although I guess none of those thoughts were my own," Peter mused.

"Actually, all of those thoughts were yours. I didn't write a script; it was more like a simulation. You still had free will and all that."

"Oh well, at least that's something," Peter said sarcastically. He looked like he was going to ask more questions, but Balthazar cut him off before he had the chance.

"Peter, believe me when I say, nothing good will come from me telling you more. I didn't tell you for your own good, or for mine. I told you because you should know. Before it's all over, you should know the truth. The world went on. That's all you really need to know about what happened after." Peter carefully considered these words from Balthazar.

"I suppose you're right." Peter looked up at Balthazar with a slight smile. "I'm still fucking pissed at you though. And I'm taking that anger with me when I go."

"I would expect nothing less. In fact, I'd be disappointed if you didn't." Balthazar returned the smile.

"So, when does it happen?" Peter asked. Balthazar stood up; a massive weight lifted.

"I've a few things to sort out first, but it'll be soon. I can't let you leave, but if you want anything, I can bring it here while you wait?" Balthazar moved to the door. Peter thought for a second, before looking at his piano.

"No. I think I'm good," Peter responded. Balthazar nodded, and left. Peter turned to his piano again. He let all those unhappy memories — all those fifteen years — float away from his mind. Becoming younger and fresher by the second. He let go of any hatred he had for Karen, and any hatred he had for any other human being. It didn't matter now. He had died at twenty-eight. He had ended it all and been stuck here ever since. None of it mattered any more.

Peter cracked his fingers and began playing. He didn't know what, and he didn't care. He just shut his eyes and let his fingers caress the keys, listening to his own music, his own sounds, for the last time.

34

Heather was caught idling as Peri approached. Before she had noticed her coming, Peri had already pulled up a chair — which hadn't existed a few seconds ago — next to Heather's desk.

"Hi again." Peri smiled.

"Uh…" Heather looked around for some help. She was under strict instructions not to speak to Peri, but she didn't hold any power here.

"Relax. Balthazar will be here any second." Peri looked over her shoulder, and right on cue, Balthazar came around the corner. Heather looked back at Peri, who was still smiling, always smiling, as Balthazar approached.

"Heather, this is Peri," Balthazar began, standing over the desk. "She's going to be working with us from now on. Well, by 'us' I don't exactly mean—"

"Ahem! Don't spoil it." Peri interrupted Balthazar, leaving Heather thoroughly confused.

"Yep, sorry." Balthazar realised in that moment he had been apologising a lot recently. He didn't like it. He turned back to Heather. "The boss is expecting me."

"Um… Yes, he is," Heather managed to blurt out. Balthazar left the two of them and went into the office. Heather looked back to Peri, who now stood.

"Let's me and you take a walk," Peri suggested. Heather was visibly hesitant; she rarely left her desk, and the last time she did was to talk to Peter which didn't exactly work out.

Peri sensed her hesitation. "It's OK, you can trust me, I have good news."

Together, they left the offices and went for a stroll. Heather was eager to know what was going on, but Peri was taking her time, taking in the surroundings like they were in a summer meadow, rather than a dull, smoking hellscape.

"I like you Heather," she said eventually.

"You don't know me," Heather replied.

"No. I don't. But my first impressions are usually correct. So, I'm trusting them," Peri clarified.

"OK. I can't really say the same," Heather offered, and Peri laughed.

"I wouldn't expect you to." They carried on walking for a while and Heather realised she would have to push the issue.

"Look. I respect the fact you're important, and you've clearly got the better of Balthazar, which doesn't happen often, but I'm too tired for games. Are we just out for a fucking walk or is there something you want to tell me?" Heather rarely cursed for fear of repercussion. But she was telling the truth, she was tired.

"OK, allow me to ask you a couple of questions first. How long have been down here?" Peri asked. Heather was hesitant to play along, but if it moved things along then she was game.

"In total? Or in my current form? Actually, I'm not sure of the answer either way," Heather admitted.

"Of course. Well, let me tell you, it's been a long time."

"No shit," Heater responded. Peri laughed again and this time Heather joined her.

"I'd say you've served your time, wouldn't you?" Peri still hadn't looked at Heather, her gaze was straight ahead, with that ever-present smile still plastered across her face.

"What do you mean?" Heather asked, confused.

"You weren't exactly the worst of the worst, Heather. Your time here would have been limited if you'd stayed in the pool. Considering the amount of time you've been put to work, I would say that your time is up." Peri stopped walking and turned to Heather. Her smile replaced by a look of sympathy that Heather had never seen before on a demon.

"What are you saying?" Heather asked, still confused.

"I've struck a deal, mainly for myself, but as a little added bonus, you've been released from service. You'll return to the pool, but you'll be immediately free," Peri explained. Heather got a little dizzy and had to steady herself on a nearby wall. If this was true, then it was everything she had been hoping for. An end to it all.

"Why are you doing this?" Heather asked, after composing herself.

"I already said, I like you. Plus, the boss is a fan of yours so this will piss him off." They both laughed again. "They'll find some other poor soul to drag into the job, but your shift is over. I hope you realise though that this means—" Peri began to explain, but Heather was quick to jump in.

"Yes. It's the end of everything. I won't exist at all after this. Believe me… I'm more than ready for that," Heater said. Peri's trademark smile returned, and they walked back towards the office together.

Once they got back to Heather's desk, Heather sat down and stared at the desk. For a long time, this had been home. For a long time, this had been all she knew. She smiled to herself as she realised; she wasn't going to miss it at all. By the time Heather looked up, Peri had disappeared.

35

Inside the devil's office, Balthazar was being prepped for everything he had to take control of while the boss was away. The boss was going through his checklist when he suddenly stopped.

"You know what, you've done this a thousand times. You know what you're doing," the devil said. He put down the paper he was holding and settled back in his throne.

"Always good to double-check. Or thousandable-check?" Balthazar kidded.

"Not sure that's a word," the boss responded with a smile.

"We're immortal beings who rule the underworld, we decide what words are." They both erupted in laughter.

"Listen, Zar, I know I haven't been great to you recently. I want you to know that's all going to change," the devil said, his tone changing. Balthazar was taken aback; he hadn't expected an apology.

"Um… yeah, I mean, no problem at all really. Happy to help."

"No, I'm serious, I've been a total dick."

"Well, you are the devil after all," Balthazar joked again.

"In name only, Zar. In name only." They both laughed again. Balthazar was happy; that couldn't have been easy for the boss to admit, but now they were comfortable again. "So, should we take care of that other matter?" The boss' eyes lit up — as did Balthazar's — they had been looking forward to this.

"Fuck yes," Balthazar replied, shifting in his seat with the excitement. The boss buzzed his intercom.

"Heather, could you bring him to us now. No warning, remember. Just like we agreed." He waited for her muffled response. "Great, thank you."

They both sat back and looked at the empty spot in the office. After a moment or two, Tantalus appeared in the office, much to his own surprise. The boss and Balthazar were doubled over with laughter, as they had interrupted Tantalus mid-wank. They watched and laughed at the shock in his eyes as he desperately pulled his pants up.

"Don't mind us Tantalus. You can finish if you want?" Balthazar joked.

"Not in my fucking office he can't. That rug is brand new!" the boss shouted, and the two of them had tears in their eyes from the laughter.

"What's going on? What's the meaning of this?" Tantalus screamed, as he wiped his hands on his trousers. The devil looked over to Balthazar.

"Would you like to do the honours?" he invited, but Balthazar shook his head.

"It should really come from you. You are still in charge after all," Balthazar replied. The devil nodded in concession.

"Good point." The devil looked over at Tantalus. "Tantalus, you're fired. You little, fucking cunt." Tantalus looked at Balthazar, hatred in his eyes, seething with every muscle till he was left twitching with rage.

"You have no idea what you're doing. I know all about your human, I know everything. I'll destroy you!" Tantalus protested. The devil looked back to Balthazar, allowing him to respond.

"Don't be so fucking dramatic Tantalus. You don't know shit. Peri threw you down the river. *We* know about *your* secret. The real one. *We* know everything. And we *could* destroy you. But we like having you around. If we get rid of you completely, someone else will take up the mantle of being the scheming little cunt. We'd rather deal with you. Better the devil you know, after all. Oh, no offense." Balthazar directed this last comment at the devil who immediately waved it off.

"None taken. Completely agreed," the devil said casually. Tantalus was incensed. He knew it was over. Not just the scheme, but everything. His work, his existence. It had all been taken away from him in an instant.

"I… this can't…" Tantalus stammered.

"One more thing Tantalus," Balthazar said, leaning forward and staring at Tantalus. "Your fly's open." Tantalus looked down to discover his fly was, in fact, not open.

“You fucking shits! I’ll—” Tantalus was gone in a flash before he could finish his empty threat. Leaving Balthazar and the boss basking in the satisfying afterglow. After a few more moments of sighing and wiping away tears, the boss looked to Balthazar, his seriousness returned.

“So then, one last bit of business,” the devil said. Balthazar avoided the boss’ gaze directly.

“Yep,” was all Balthazar could muster.

“You know, you don’t have to do it yourself?” he offered, but Balthazar was resolute.

“No, no. I brought him out — and then some — I should be the one to put him back.” The boss simply nodded, and they sat in silence for a minute or two, as the weight of his next task dropped heavily onto Balthazar’s mind and body. He shook himself out of it and turned his attention back to his boss.

“What’s next for you? With the insomnia thing?” he asked.

The devil shrugged a little, he hadn’t really thought about it yet. “I’m not sure there is a next. Maybe I’ll retire, and you and Peri can run things from now on,” he said casually. “Or maybe I’ll just exercise more,” he added, with a wink.

36

Peter sat up in his bed and looked around his room. He had stayed in worse places, like friends' couches and cheap hotels. He wasn't even sure this place ranked in the top five of the worst places he'd stayed in. Peter had slept heavily and freely. The last fifteen years of his life had evaporated into the mist. He still remembered them; they were as clear as the rocks and the fire burning around him. But the memories had lost their impact. No longer did they torture him, no longer could they reach out to him in the night and disturb his sleep.

Balthazar awoke that morning with a severe sense of dread that hung over him like a raincloud. He looked around his room. It was still his. His space, his comfort, his life. Things were turning around and looking up. This place would always be his, it would always be home. On this morning however, the fire burned lower, the smell fainter, and the familiar rocky edges grew smoother as the room warped itself to mirror his own despair. Breathing deeply, Balthazar got up, got his head straight, and left.

When he arrived, Peter was already awake and sitting anxiously on the bed. They said nothing in greeting, Peter simply got up, and together, they walked out. Peter looked back at the room as he was leaving, for the last time, and saw the Baby Grand piano slowly fall to dust. Peter wondered if the same fate met his fleshlight, but not wishing to witness a plastic vagina disintegrating as his last memory, he chose not to look for it.

"So, is there a literal pool that we're going to?" Peter asked, he wasn't really curious, any curiosity he had left vanished yesterday. He was asking to fill the silence, which was deafening.

"Not exactly. It's not a physical location per se. But there is a place we use to represent it. That's where we're going," Balthazar explained.

"Interesting. So, there won't be a bunch of dead souls swimming around while their very essence fades away?"

"Fuck no. That would be a bit grim wouldn't it?"

"Yep, it certainly would be," Peter replied and they both smiled sadly. They walked on in silence for a little while. Peter knew by now that they could instantly get to wherever they were going. They were walking for a reason. Balthazar was giving Peter some more time. Last night, he had resolved himself not to say anything, to let his mind go blank and enjoy his final walk. Now that they were here though, Peter felt compelled to say something.

"Balthazar, I'll never forgive you," Peter said quietly. Balthazar did not stop, but he slowed down noticeably, and they walked on. "I don't know if you care about that. Or if it really matters given where I'm going. But I still want you to know. I want you to know that I'll never forgive you." Peter paused for a moment, allowing the weight of his words to fall on Balthazar. "I don't blame you. I'm not still angry, I'm not still upset. Frankly, we're good. And if I were sticking around, we'd have no issues. But I will never forgive you," Peter finished. He had been looking ahead the whole time but now he side-eyed Balthazar to see his reaction, which was minimal.

"I understand," Balthazar finally said. "And that's my cross to bear."

"Interesting choice of words," Peter replied, and they both laughed.

Finally, they arrived at something akin to a waterfall. It was the closest real world thing Peter could compare it to. There was no water though, at least not in the traditional sense. There was a flow of something that barely appeared to be liquid, and it was flowing over a cliff face and into a murky valley below them. Peter took some deep breaths.

"What do we do now?" he asked. But Balthazar was looking over his shoulder. Peter turned to see Heather standing with another figure that he didn't recognise.

"Not quite yet Peter. I have to do this first."

"Heather's going back to the pool?" Peter asked.

"No, she's served her time. She's going away, for good," Balthazar explained. Peter looked at Heather again, who looked back and smiled. Peter waved. He wasn't sure why; he didn't know what the correct etiquette was when you were standing on the edge of existence and mortality. Balthazar walked over to Heather and Peri. He smiled at Peri and looked at Heather.

"Ready?" he asked her. Heather couldn't speak but she nodded. Peri put a hand on her shoulder, and they shared a look. Giving Balthazar one last smile, Peri walked away. Peter watched on as Balthazar and Heather stared at each other. It didn't appear that anything was happening, and Peter was about to move closer when suddenly, Heather's figure began to dissipate. Slowly, as if atom-by-atom, the pieces of her floated away and fell into the valley below. When there was nothing left, Balthazar turned slowly and walked back to Peter.

"That's really how it happens? We slowly fade away like the end of movie?" Peter asked, incredulous.

"No. Don't be fucking stupid. The effect is instantaneous. All that is just a little trick, you know? A bit of flair, makes it all dramatic and shit." Balthazar waved his hands in explanation. Peter shook his head and laughed.

"I guess I never got the hang of the place."

"You're not the first and you won't be last, Peter."

"So, who was that person anyway? Something going on there?" Peter raised his eyebrows in jest.

"Shut the fuck up, Peter."

"That's a yes. You guys do it yet?" Peter smiled, and Balthazar returned it.

"A pervert to the very fucking end," Balthazar joked, and they laughed. "Let's not worry about me right now," Balthazar said, returning to the matter at hand.

"Of course." Peter looked up at Balthazar and said, "OK, let's do it." Balthazar sighed heavily.

"There's one more thing Peter."

"For fuck's sake. There's always one more thing." Peter said, exasperated. Balthazar held a hand up to silence Peter. It was the same hand he used that first meeting, back in the café. It still held its power.

"Peter this is serious. Those last fifteen years, the years I gave you. You don't have to take them with you. I can take them away, and you can return, to live out your existence with only your real life as memory." Balthazar put his hand down as he finished his proposition.

Peter forcibly blinked a few times as the words reached him. He hadn't thought of this before. He could go back. Back to his late twenties. Back to the end of his marriage. No miserable thirties, no lonely years spent uninspired, writing jingles for his cousin. He could go back. Back to the man who went through with it.

Balthazar watched as Peter's eyes darted back and forth in deep consideration. His face changed, his brow furrowed, and his mouth tightened. Then he looked up.

"No," Was all Peter said. Balthazar was somewhat surprised.

"No?" Balthazar felt he had to clarify.

"You're the one always telling me Balthazar, nothing is real down here. I think it's the same up there. That fake life you gave me was fucking awful but it was as real as the one I actually had — which was also fucking awful. The point is, what does it matter? What does it matter how those memories got there? Where they came from? How I lived that life? It was all real to me. It's all part of who I am *now*," Peter explained. Balthazar looked at him, he had grown to like him over their time together, but for the first time, Balthazar felt he respected him. Not as a human, or a friend, but as a being. As a figure of conscience and consciousness.

"OK then. Peter, you're going back to serve the rest of your time. Under the circumstances it felt right to give you a reduced sentence. So, it's not forever, more like infinity minus a week or two."

"Well, that makes all the difference," Peter joked. Balthazar placed a hand on his shoulder.

"Goodbye, Peter," Balthazar said, with sadness in his eyes. As Peter felt his physical being slip away, he looked up at Balthazar and smiled.

"Goodbye, Balthazar," he said, as he faded out of existence.

Balthazar was left alone, standing next to the valley. He looked down at the murky depths and considered his own future. There was no end for him, it almost made him jealous of humans… almost. All he could do was keep going. Maybe the boss would retire, and he would be handed the throne. Maybe he wouldn't accept it, and pass it on to Peri, where he would continue his role as right-hand man. Maybe she would love him back and they would rule together till the whole place froze over. Balthazar walked away from the edge, taking excitement from not knowing. The future would be whatever the fuck he wanted it to be, and right now, he wanted to get some fucking rest. *We all need some rest after all,* he thought.